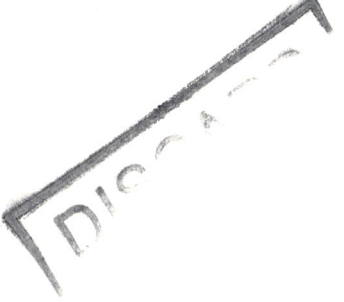

The Black Sheriff

Because he is black, lawman Otis McGee suffers a close brush with Judge Lynch after a young white girl, Eunice Thark, is found raped outside the township of Tulsa. How can he escape the angry mob and trace the real assailant?

Otis has other problems, too. A wildcat oilman, busy cheating the Osage Indians out of their land rights, has reasons for wanting McGee dead. Then, a gang of homicidal desperadoes, who snatch bawdy-house girls for use as human shields, is also after his blood. How can Otis outgun or outwit them? How can he save the dead girl's beautiful twin, Violet, from a similar fate to that of her sister?

The praised writer, John Dyson, has created another dazzling western which will enhance his growing reputation.

The Black Sheriff

JOHN DYSON

A Black Horse Western

ROBERT HALE · LONDON

© John Dyson 2001
First published in Great Britain 2001

ISBN 0 7090 6794 1

Robert Hale Limited
Clerkenwell House
Clerkenwell Green
London EC1R 0HT

Typeset by Derek Doyle & Associates, Liverpool.
Printed and bound in Great Britain by
Antony Rowe Limited, Wiltshire.

One

To ride by night was never a good idea, especially on a wild night like this when a sliver of moon was generally concealed by dark and rolling rain clouds. But Otis McGee was in a hurry and had spurred his mustang on through the darkness at a hard lope. A foreleg down a prairie fox hole, a snap of bone, a squealing whinny of pain and horse and rider were sent rolling and tumbling to hit the ground hard. Otis was winded for some moments, his breath gurgling from him, but he picked himself up, brushed himself down, and groped around for his wide-brimmed black "preacher's" hat. The mustang, though, was in a bad way – struggling to his feet, attempting to hobble on three legs, the broken bone protruding through skin.

'Hail, ole fella,' Otis tut-tutted. 'I'se afraid you come to the end of the trail. Don't feel bad about this, but there ain't nuthin' else for it.'

He uncinched the saddle, his carbine and bedroll, and tried to soothe the animal as he unbuckled the bridle, tossing it aside. He drew a long-barrelled Colt Frontier from the shoulder-hung holster beneath his suit jacket, clicked the cylinder around, pressed the barrel to the beast's temple, and fired. He listened to the reverberation of the shot through the darkness and watched the mustang tumble to the ground. '*Adios, amigo,*' he whispered.

Slenderly built, Otis did not relish hefting the saddle rig, bedroll and his high-powered Creedmore carbine, .44-100 calibre, on his shoulders to the nearest town. He was unsure just how far that might be in this poorly-mapped Indian Territory. He had been following the north bank of the Arkansas River, but there might well be streams to cross. So he left his gear in some rocks by the dead horse and headed on his way. 'Once I git myself a new bronc I'll come back for it,' he muttered. 'It's gonna be tough enough footin' it. These damn high-heel boots weren't made for walkin'.'

Two hours and ten miles of hard walking later, he heard the drawn-out wail of a locomotive's steam siren. It was probably an offshoot of the main Atchison Topeka and Santa Fe line which crossed Kansas to the north. Small railroads had begun to criss-cross the territory.

Otis trudged on and saw a sign – 'Tulsa Town, pop. 203' – and the mouth of a mining shaft, with gantry and wheels alongside a big pile of slag. Beyond were the shadowy shapes of clapboard houses and false fronts clustered on both sides of a muddy main street through which a single-track iron railroad passed. It was a working town, a tang of coaldust everywhere, devoid of life in these early hours of the morning except for a rib-thin stray hound that ran up barking and snarling.

'Must be some kinda mining town,' Otis said as he strode along past a darkened saloon, a general store, a forge, livery and flour mill with its three-storey warehouse. The only sounds were the wind banging a loose shutter, and the whimpering of the dog at his heels.

Alongside the line on the far side of town was a little telegraph and booking office. There was a small waiting room, with a pot-bellied coal stove still glowing warm. So Otis settled down on a wooden bench. 'Don't go cosying up to me, son,' he growled at the liver-coloured hound. 'I ain't got nuthin'.' He tipped his hat over his eyes, folded his arms, stuck out his legs to rest on the spurs of his boots, and settled down to doze. 'It's jest my damn fine luck, ain't it?' he muttered before he drifted off into dark and haunted dreams.

'Okay, boy, don't make a move. You hold it right there.'

Otis woke with a start to find daylight in his eyes, and saw a spindleshanks of a railroadman holding a double-barrelled twelve-gauge against his chest, poking at the black fella's revolver beneath his coat.

'He's got a gun hidden under his coat,' the railroadman wheezed. 'Soon as I see'd him I knew it must be him. Thass why I come runnin' to git ya.'

'You did right, Jim.' A bald-headed man with a barrel girth, a checked shirt tucked into baggy pants, themselves tucked into riding boots, was standing studying him, chewing at a plug of baccy which bulged out one cheek. 'You did right. He's the one it must be. You git ready to blast him to Kingdom Come if he makes a false move. You, son, take that piece out by the butt in two fingers real slow.' The fat man pulled his own six-shooter from the thick leather belt around his flabby, gut, aimed it unfalteringly at Otis, thumbing the hammer. 'You ready, Jim?'

'Sure am, Sheriff. It won't be the first time I kilt a nigra.'

Otis's dark-eyed gaze flickered over the tin star pinned to the fat man's shirt and up to challenge the little eyeholes in a face that had the lumpy texture of a burned potato.

'What's this all about, Sheriff? Tell your itchy-fingered friend to take it easy. I ain't lookin' for no trouble.' He did as he was bid, carefully removing the Frontier from beneath the jacket of his black suit 'twixt forefinger and thumb. 'There y'are. Man's entitled to carry a gun, ain't he?'

'Lay it on the floor. Careful now, we're watching you.' As Otis did so, the sheriff kicked the revolver aside towards the stove and the curled-up hound, who jumped and regarded the men mournfully, as if annoyed at being disturbed from his slumber. 'Right, stranger. Now you stand up, face the wall, put your hands behind you.'

'Aw, come on, Sheriff,' Otis grinned, opening his palms, pleadingly. 'You gone got me all wrong.'

The fat man continued to chew at his baccy plug, and spat a brown gob to splat Otis's boot. 'You damn bastard. You do what I tell you, pronto.'

Otis got to his feet, towering over them, and shrugged, turning to the wall, putting his hands behind him. The railroadman jabbed the shotgun in his side as the sheriff snapped handcuffs on his wrists. 'You're making a mistake,' Otis drawled as the sheriff frisked him, taking the knife from the sheath on his belt.

'That must be the murder weapon,' the man called Jim whooped. 'See them bloodstains on it?'

'Those bloodstains are from a jack-rabbit I gutted for supper. Guess I shoulda cleaned it better.'

'You sure should,' Jim yelled, excitedly, ''specially when you done use it to slit a white woman's throat.'

'What in hail's he talkin' 'bout?' Otis turned back, angrily, to face them. 'I know nuthin' about no white woman.'

'What's a coloured boy like you doing in these parts?' the sheriff drawled, chewing some more, languidly. 'Where you from, boy?'

'Wild Cat, thass my town. Not far outa Fort Gibson. I'm a freed slave. A freedman. I can go where I like, cain't I? Ain't that what your war was all about?'

'What's a black like you doing in Indian Territory?' Jim challenged, the shotgun still gripped in his hands.

'I was a slave of the Chickasaws, dimbrain, before the war. There's hundreds of us. This is our country now as well as yours.'

'Wild Cat? Ain't that one of them coloured townships, like Tullahassee, this side of the Arkansas border?' the sheriff asked.

'Thass right.' Otis McGee's eyes glowed with fierce pride, his face stern, his muscled neck in dark contrast with his white collarless shirt. 'So happens I'm my town's sheriff.'

'Haw! Who's he tryin' to kid?' Jim scoffed. 'These blacks'll try anythang to wriggle out the noose. We're gonna string you high, mister. But 'fore that we're gonna whup you and brand you.'

'You'll find my badge in my jacket pocket.'

'What's it doin' there?' The sheriff dipped in his fist and came up with the star. 'Why aincha wearing it?'

'Because I'm on the trail of some badmen and it ain't always wise to proclaim who you are when you walk into a saloon.'

'You hear that, Brick? That's piffle!' Jim hooted. 'He probably killed some lawman and stole that. Got rapist writ all over him, the ugly—'

'All right, Jim, simmer down.' Sheriff Brick Brady frowned as the railroadman began cursing and hurling racist insults. 'I'm handling this. We got him. He'll get a proper trial and a lawful hanging. Don't go stirring folks up.'

'Aw, come off it,' Otis pleaded. 'Telegraph Fort Gibson or Fort Smith. They'll confirm who I am.'

'So, who are you?'

'Sheriff Otis McGee.'

'Yeah, how can they confirm anythang without seein' ya?' Jim put in. 'You coulda stole his badge and his name. He's the only one it could be, Brick. You been out all night combing the whole area, aincha? Who else you come up with?'

'Yep, looks like you're the chief suspect, mister. Git moving. I'm marching you down to the hoosegow.'

Prodded by the railroadman's twelve gauge, Otis had no option but to stride down the muddy main street towards the town jail. The town of Tulsa had suddenly come to life, shopkeepers opening their shutters, white women in figure-muffling clothes sweeping their porches and sidewalks, a barber outside his shop, a man harnessing a mule to a wagon, pausing to stare.

'We got him!' Jim shrieked to one and all. 'I found him hidin' in my waitin' room. We got Eunice Thark's murderer.'

'For God's sake!' Otis shouted, as a crowd, mostly women, ran to gather around them, hissing and catcalling, their clawlike fingers reaching out to tear at his clothing, galvanized by righteous anger that a black should have some such vile things to a white girl. 'Why don't you tell him to shut up? Why doncha tell 'em who I am, Sheriff?'

'You'll git to say your bit in court.' Sheriff Brady shielded the black man with his brawny arms, fighting through the mob, hurling Otis into his jailhouse, turning to block the doorway. 'That's enough,' he roared. 'Nothing ain't proven yet. I got investigations to make. Go away. Go back to your shops, to your work, your homes. This man's my prisoner an' I'm keeping him safe 'til his trial.'

'What are you, a nigra lover?' a woman screamed and spat in the sheriff's face. 'Damn you to hell.'

Sheriff Brady stepped back and slammed the door in her face, locking and barring it. He turned to Otis and for the first time gave a scoffing grin, wiping the spittle from his face. 'I guess that was meant for you.'

He signalled Otis to step into a cell and turned the key in the barred door. 'I guess you could do with a coffee. So could I. I been out with the posse all night looking for you. Howja like it' – he grinned again as he put the pot on the stove – 'black?'

'Black's good enough.' Otis listened to a fist hammering the door and people's shouts outside as the news was passed on. 'Those folks sure got blood lust. All I was figuring was to wait 'til daylight and buy myself a hoss. Looks like I walked into a hornets' nest.'

'It sure does.' Sheriff Brady scratched at his shirt, nervously. 'To tell the truth, boy, things don't look good. I ain't sure I can hold these people off. Eunice Thark was a popular girl, the town schoolteacher. Very modest, very pretty, a lot of men were fond of her. You shoulda seen her when we found her, raped and beaten, not a nice sight. I seen a few stiffs in my time but I very near brought up my supper.'

Otis sat on his bunk and pondered his predicament for a while. He was well aware of lynch law. He knew what happened when white folks got het up. He had seen black bodies hanging from the trees before now. His chances did not look good. He accepted the tin cup of black coffee passed through the bars and said, 'This Eunice Thark? Did she have any menfriends? When and where was she found?'

'Hey, McGee, you really are pretending to be innocent, aincha? You know very well where she was found. Out on the trail, dragged from her buggy, left for dead.'

'Who found her? What time?'

'An elderly rancher and his wife in their wagon on their way home. It must have been about nine o'clock last night. Her body was still warm.'

'Well, I was nowhere near this damn town.'

'Yeah? Tell that to the judge and jury. They'll be sure to believe ya, same as me. Why doncha just confess, McGee? You saw this beaut of a white woman driving her buggy. You wanted her. And you brutally and foully had your way. Tell the truth, boy. It'll save us all a lot of time.'

'What about my second question? Did she have a fella?'

'What's that got to do with you?'

'Aincha heard, Sheriff? Drunken domestic disputes or jealous passion accounts for twenty-five per cent of the cases where wimmin end up dead.'

'Don't get smart with me, boy. Who the hell you think you are, trying to tell me my job?' Brady angrily spat out the remains of his baccy plug, missing the brass spittoon. 'So happens the gentleman Miss Thark was engaged to is above suspicion. So you just keep your nose outa this.'

Sheriff Brady ambled over to his desk and began opening and banging closed drawers like an angry bear. 'Where in tarnation did that whiskey git to? I need a slug. I been out all night.'

'Yeah, so've I,' Otis growled. 'You been out to interview this noble gentleman who's above suspicion?'

'I tell ya,' Brady shouted. 'There's no need to. Carol Lindeman owns this town, the railroad, the mine, and me, too; he can rig the votes that keep me in or put me outa office.'

'So that means you're gonna let him get off if he shoulda done this thing?'

'No. I'm saying he's the kind of man who couldn't have done this. I know that for a fact.'

'An' he's so damn powerful he'll be expecting you to come up with the kind of man who might have – like a negro? He's gonna want swift so-called justice an' the sooner I'm hanged with few questions asked the better it'll be.'

'It ain't like that, so don't you go trying to make out it is. You're the chief suspect, not Mister Lindeman.' Brady finally located his bottle under a dusty, rarely-opened law book where he'd hidden it out of the way of his thieving deputy. 'Ah,' he sighed, pulling the cork and taking a swig. 'Thass the stuff.'

'I might be your chief suspect, you fat, lazy, drunken, dishonest bastard,' Otis roared, 'but I got an alibi. The night before this last one I took a room in the Hotel Grotto at Redwood. I played poker with none other than George Maledon.'

'The territorial hangman?'

'Yup. Why don't you send a wire to the hotel to verify that? The night clerk signed me out at four a.m. I rode all through the day, changed horses at Okmugee, and rode on through the night. My bronc broke a leg an' I did the last ten miles on foot. The booking hall clock said 4.30 a.m. when I got here. I'd been travellin' for twenty-four hours non-stop to try to make time on those men I was pursuing. No man coulda got here faster unless his hoss sprouted wings an' flew. There's no way I coulda been outside this town rapin' an' murderin' at eight or nine p.m. last night.'

Brady stared at the fast-talking black man with

wonderment. 'You sure got the gift of the gab, aincha, boy? Let's get this straight. You claim you left Redwood at four yesterday morning?'

'Thass the God's honest truth,' Otis sang out. 'I was twenty-four hours from Tulsa.'

'Yeah,' Sheriff Brady butted in. 'Maybe I'll check on that.' He got to his feet and swaggered over, offering the bottle through the bars. 'You wanna pull?'

'No. Never touch the demon drink these days. I seen what it does to men. Thanks all the same.'

'Please yourself,' Brady said, somewhat miffed. 'There ain't many men I offer my whiskey to.'

'Any chance of taking a look at the body?'

'What?' Brady roared. 'You really got some nerve, boy. What are you, some kinda ghoul?'

'Her body might give us some clue as to how she come to be that way. You must know that, Sheriff.'

Brady finished the dregs of the bottle and tossed it clattering into a corner. 'You think I'm gonna let some black boy gloat over the naked body of a white gal?' He bellowed like a rutting buffalo. 'You really want to git folks riled up?'

'It wouldn't be to gloat.' Otis stared at him, solemnly. 'It would be in the interests of justice. Black or white don't make no difference to me. A stiff's a stiff.'

Brady tipped his hat over his eyes and scratched the back of his bald head. 'You know, McGee, you sure are some weird guy.' He looked around, furtively, glancing through the cobwebbed glass of his barred office window. 'It so happens we got her laid out in the next room. Brought her in last night.

Ain't had time to contact the undertaker yet.'

'So nobody'll be the wiser.'

'True.' Brady took his keys from a hook and began to unlock. 'You give me your word you ain't gonna try any funny tricks?'

'Cross my heart,' Otis grinned. 'Lead on, man.'

The sheriff let him out, his revolver cocked and ready in his fist as a precaution, and unlocked another door to a dimly lit room. He gave a gasp when he caught the whiff of decaying flesh and pulled his neckerchief over his mouth. 'A corpse don't keep long in this heat. Sooner we get her planted the better.'

'Yeah,' Otis muttered, stepping closer to the dead body of a young woman of about twenty-three years, who, it was obvious, had been beautiful, lissom and well-formed not long before; but now her blonde hair hung back from her bludgeoned skull and her features had been trapped in a rictal snarl of pain, like some wild animal, probably when she had received the slash across her neck. Livor mortis had quickly set in causing a reddish-purple discoloration of the skin, and by now rigor mortis, the stiffening of the muscles, was fully established. Eunice Thark was dressed in a skirt and blouse but they had been torn apart as if in some violent struggle. Otis peered at her right hand. One of the nails was torn half off. 'She didn't give in without a struggle. Somebody somewhere's got a pretty bad scratch, probably across his face.'

The girl's hands had been tanned by the sun, but there was a white circle on one finger. 'Looks like her attacker stole her ring. You don't happen to remember her wearing it, Sheriff? What it was like, by any chance?'

'I don't go round looking at women's jewellery,' Brady replied. 'Hang on, I do remember she always wore some kinda Indian charm on a silver chain around her neck. It was made of green jade, flat and egg-shaped, a kinda squatting half-man, half-animal god, you know the kinda stuff the Cherokee carve. Yes, she always wore it. I asked about it once. She said her father gave it her for good luck.'

'Well, it didn't bring much of that. And it certainly ain't there now.'

'Wait a minute!' Brady stared in disbelief as the black prisoner pulled apart the girl's torn and muddy skirt and put his hands on her upper thighs. 'What 'n hell you doin'? Take your hands off her, you dirty—'

'Shut up, Brady. Don't talk more stupid than you act. I'm examining her body. She ain't wearing pantalettes. Did you find them at the scene?'

'No, we didn't. Hey, you cain't do that. You ain't a doctor.'

'She's badly swollen and scratched. I'd say there was some violent intercourse.'

'That was obvious the way she was lying. Cover her up. Have some respect.'

Otis did so, and bent to examine her face. As well as the bloody contusion to her temple, and the throat slash, there was a gash across her left cheek going upwards towards the bridge of the nose. 'I'd say a ring with a sharp stone did that. Somebody wearing one gave her a vicious backhander.'

'Come on.' Brady's nose twitched, distastefully. 'You seen enough, aincha?'

'Yes,' he whispered, touching her cheek, gently. 'Poor kid. Still, you've got a couple of clues now.'

'I guess. Man with a scratch on his face. Say, that's a pretty bad scratch you got.'

'That happened when my hoss took a tumble. Come on, Sheriff. How about you go wire Redwood? I need to be on my way. Those boys I'm after will be well away by now.'

As they returned to the sheriff's office, both men jumped with alarm as a rock was hurled through the front window with a crashing of glass, and they heard yells and curses outside.

'There he is!' a man yelled. 'Bring him out, Sheriff. We want him.'

'What in tarnation!' Sheriff Brady jumped back against the wall. 'Git on the floor, McGee. They can see you.'

Otis hurled himself down as another rock shattered the remains of the window. He rolled over to the far wall, and there was fear in the white of his eyes as he looked across. There was no man living who wouldn't be in fear of a lynch mob. 'How about returning my revolver, Sheriff?' he called. 'I'm gonna need to defend myself.'

'No need for that. I can handle this.' Brady bit his lip, considering, then crawled across to the window, poking his own revolver through the bars and peering out. 'This is Sheriff Brady speaking,' he bellowed. 'I am by no means convinced this prisoner is guilty. He claims to be a lawman from Wild Cat. Whatever, if you people don't disperse by the time I count ten I'm gonna start shooting. I ain't having no mob rule in my town. Be warned, if you try to harm my prisoner you are committing treason against the constitution. I have the right under the Riot Act to bear arms against you. Is that understood?'

'Go to hell, Brady,' a big, husky miner at the front of the crowd yelled. ''You wouldn't dare. Give us the nigra or we'll burn you down.'

'Don't tempt me. I'm starting counting.'

But his words only seemed to enrage the mob more. Men and women surged forwards in a mass, red-faced and angry, screaming and jeering, until they were a few feet from the broken window. The big, bearded miner, whom Brady had his revolver levelled at, was pushed forwards, a tad unwillingly now, but he had a stout rope with a noose in his hands. He brandished it and called out, 'You cain't shoot us all down in cold blood, Brady. We've got plenty dynamite. We'll blow your jailhouse to Kingdom Come.'

'I'm counting!' Brady shouted, but he looked by no means certain that he could carry out his threat. He wiped sweat from his eyes and the six-gun trembled in his fist. 'You people must see sense. I don't want no bloodshed.'

Otis, watching, knew that Brady would not go through with it and that, eventually, he would surrender. He hadn't got the guts to fire on his own kind for some black man. So, he reached up to a rifle rack and helped himself to a Spencer carbine, swinging it down, and quietly checking to see if it was loaded. It was. He levered a slug out of the magazine into the breech. 'Nobody's hanging me,' he hissed.

But, suddenly, there were more alarmed cries from outside, and he sidled across to crouch beside the sheriff at the window. Six men on horseback were riding into the mob, cracking lariats across their backs, breaking them up. 'Har! Hyah!' they hollered, as if they were cutting out cattle. 'Git back!'

They had forced a pathway through the crowd and through that came riding a dark-bearded gentleman in a pearl grey suit, low-crowned hat and long duster coat. His mount was a fine grey thoroughbred and his saddle horn and bridle flashed with silver in the sun. 'What's going on?' he snapped out.

The big-chested ringleader turned to him, obviously protesting, but talking in some strange Slavonic language. Carol Lindeman, for it must be he, replied in kind, and shouted, 'Get back to the mine. I'm not paying you for this. Any of you want to argue you can get out.'

Reluctantly, growling like whipped dogs, the crowd backed off and broke up, the men and their few women hangers-on skulking away to watch from a distance as Lindeman dismounted and called out, 'All right, Brady, you can open up. Let's take a look at this prisoner of yours.'

Brady glanced across at the black sheriff, who was standing poised facing the door, the Spencer in readiness in his hands. 'Don't do it, McGee,' he said. 'Put that back in the rack. I'll git you outa this mess somehow.'

Otis hesitated, then put the carbine aside and

stepped back into his cell, closing the barred door.

'Jeez!' he gasped, with a grin. 'I got the feel of a hempen necktie round my throat. That was a close call.'

'You ain't outa this yet,' Brady muttered. 'Our friend out there is still gonna try to hang ya, but by legal means, thass for sure.' He grunted as he unlocked the jailhouse door, allowing Lindeman and two of his bodyguards to step in. 'Howdy, sir. You arrived in the nick of time. This here's the prisoner. And Eunice's body is in the other room. It sure is a terrible thing.'

TWO

'We can't hold him, Mistuh Lindeman,' Brady said. 'He seems to have got a cast iron alibi. I've telegraphed Redwood to verify. I'm expecting a reply any time now. He's a lawman, to boot.'

'A black lawman? I didn't know there was such a thing.'

'Oh, yeah, Marshal Bass Reeves has done good work for ten years now outa Fort Smith. He helped put down the Dalton boys. And there's other black sheriffs in the coloured towns.'

'Plenty of lawmen have been known to go to the bad.' The suave Lindeman twitched one nostril, disdainfully. He was immaculately attired, with a clipped beard and thick, neatly-parted wedges of hair, and was of the middle-European Slavonic race. He studied Otis through the bars and said, 'I'm not so sure this bird is as innocent as he pretends. I want this terrible matter thoroughly investigated, Brady.'

'You mean you want me to hold him?'

'You can't do that,' Otis protested. 'It ain't legal.'

'I can do what I like in this town,' Carol Lindeman replied, drawing fastidiously on a thin cigar and blowing smoke in Otis's direction. 'Be thankful you're still alive. But you're still our main suspect and I'm going to press for trial.'

'Rubbish,' Otis growled. 'In my book, if I was looking into this murder, you'd be my main suspect. You cain't hold me, so unlock this cage and I'll be on my way.'

'Me? Main suspect?' Lindeman looked startled for the first time. 'What on earth are you talking about, man?'

'You were the lady's fancy man, weren't ya? You had given her a ring, promised marriage? As I understand it she drove her buggy out to your mining camp about six miles from town. So – did you have a quarrel? What happened to the engagement ring that was on her finger?'

'McGee, you can't question Mistuh Lindeman like this. Who you think you are?' Brady cautioned. 'You ain't got the right. Mistuh Lindeman ain't a suspect in my book. No way. As for the ring, obviously the rapist would have stole it. Find the ring, we find him.'

'That's all right, Brady, I'll answer this black's insulting questions, even if I won't forget them in a hurry. As it happens we did argue. Eunice was a very emotional woman. When I told her that I had to break off our engagement, that I intended to marry another girl, she got into a terrible temper and hurled the ring at me. It missed and landed in the brush somewhere. I did not bother to seek it out because Eunice had jumped onto her buggy and set off at quite a pace back towards town.'

'You didn't go after her?' Otis demanded. 'You

didn't consider it dangerous for her to be out alone that time of night?'

'No, it was still daylight. It was only a short drive. I was upset, too. I knew if I went after her there would be tears and recriminations, she would try to persuade me to change my mind. I decided to let her go. I wish now, of course, that I had gone after her. I bitterly regret the whole thing. But what's done is done.'

'A schoolmarm don't earn a lot. She ain't got much of a future 'cept becoming some old spinster. I guess Eunice was happy to be marrying a rich man, a railroad and mine-owner. I guess she *was* upset. But, if I may say so, it don't seem to bother you that much.'

'I'm not a man who shows his feelings, but believe me I'm shocked and hurting inside. I've vowed to see that whoever took this poor girl's life will be put on trial and hanged. I mean that.'

'This poor gal – is that all she was to you?'

'Look, McGee, or whatever you call yourself, I don't like your insolent tone. But I'll tell you the truth. Eunice and I were lovers. I told her we could still be, but I had to marry another . . . for business reasons. She took it badly.'

'Well,' Otis smiled, 'I guess she would. *Sorry, honey, I cain't marry ya, but I kin still see ya on the side—*'

'Cut the crap,' Lindeman snapped. 'Is there anything else you want to know?'

'Yes. Who is this new lady love of yours? And why the business reasons? She got money by any chance?'

'No.' Lindeman looked irritated, and stubbed out

the cigar beneath his heel. 'I suppose *you* ought to be asking these sort of questions, Brady, so I'll clear the air. It's gonna be public knowledge soon, anyhow. My new fiancée is an Indian girl. Her father is a chief among the Osage nation.'

'Ah, I get it,' Otis grinned. 'An' if you marry her this'll give you the right by federal law to mine coal on their lands.'

'No, not coal. Oil. I'm looking to the future. I'll continue mining coal, of course. But I've already formed a new company: the Lindeman Gasoline and Petroleum Company. It's going to be big.'

'Oil? That greasy black stuff? What good's that?' Otis asked, genuinely puzzled.

'Heating, lighting, driving industrial machines, all kinds of things. So now you know. Does that clear me?'

'Not necessarily. But I guess it explains a few things. You sure you didn't send a couple of your iron-hung thugs after her' – Otis glanced at two of the bodyguards, not miners, but hard men, in leather chaps and range clothes, who lounged against the walls watching and listening – 'they caught up with her and things got outa hand?'

'If they had touched her they would be dead by now,' Lindeman snarled, a pained look in his dark eyes. 'But no, I did not send them after her. Right, I think I have said all I need to.'

'Just one more thing,' Otis called, as the mine owner sprang to his feet. 'Thass a fancy diamond ring you wear on your left hand. Eunice Thark was back-handed across her left cheek by a left-handed man wearing a ring like that. Are you left-handed by any chance?'

'You—' Lindeman hissed. 'You've got a damned nerve. How dare you speak to me like that. I ought to have let the mob have their way. No, I'm not left-handed. I'm ambidextrous, if you must know.'

He stepped out, his cronies clattering after him, slamming the door.

'You've certainly put his nose out of joint,' Brady muttered. 'Not a wise thing to do, Otis. You could be signing your own death warrant. You're too damn cocky for your own good.'

'Wake up, McGee, I got you some grub.' Sheriff Brick Brady shouted at some men hanging about outside to clear off as he hurriedly squeezed through the jail-house door, slammed it shut and locked it. He had a tray of hot food in his hand which he shoved through an aperture in the bars. 'Folks still prowling about outside like damn wolves with their tongues hung out slavering for blood.'

'Yeah.' Otis had been trying to get some sleep during the long day for he had been on the trail twenty-four hours and needed some. But his cat doze had been constantly disturbed by men, women, even children, coming to peer through the broken office window, jeering, cursing, threatening that they were going to break in and get him, that he would never get out of town alive. 'They didn't let me git much shut-eye.'

Brady poured coffee into a tin cup and passed it through to him. 'Most of 'em wouldn't ordinarily go against Mistuh Lindeman's wishes. He pays their wages. But you never know when a fidgety mob might explode. I don't like it.'

'How you think I feel?' Otis carved up the ham and eggs and ate hungrily, stuffing bread into his mouth. It was late afternoon and his first meal of the day. 'You taken your time over this, aincha? Ain't you heard of prisoners' rights? Thought you were gonna let me starve to death.'

'I been busy. I went to look at the scene of the crime in the daylight, but there ain't nuthin', just a lot of hoofprints in the mud.'

'A lot of hoofprints?'

'Yeah, milling around, but I couldn't make nuthin' out. I followed some of the tracks up river a fair way to the shallows, but they petered out t'other side. Those boys you were following, who were they?'

'Jed Flinn's gang. Meanest bunch of varmints you're ever likely to come across.' Otis gulped a mouthful down, wiped grease from his jaw, and frowned. 'Flinn's a whiteman, lean, tall, thin-jawed, wanted for bustin' outa Arkansas state prison along with his pal, a piece of white trash called Charlie Gilpatrick. Both psychopaths. I should know, I put 'em there for horse-thieving and homicide.'

'Are they all white?'

'No.' Otis wiped up the egg yolk with his bread. 'They've been joined by a black boy, Eli Gritts, who used to live in Wild Cat, but left home and went to the bad. And, you heard of Blue Duck, notorious bank-robber, rustler? A full-blood Cherokee, dresses flash like a whiteman in a three-piece suit. Only difference is he wears a feather in his high-bowled hat. He's with 'em.'

'Yep, I've had some Wanted notices come through on him.'

Otis took a sip of the coffee and nodded. 'The fifth member of the gang's a Choctaw breed with a fancy name, Theophilus Tadpole. A minor ne'er-do-well who ain't in the same league as Flinn and Blue Duck, at least not until now.'

'Why you after them, McGee?'

'They paid my town a visit three days ago. Wild Cat, in spite of its name, is generally a quiet, industrious coloured town. Most folks work on their farms growin' tobacco or cotton. We got a big tobacco ware-house where it's processed to ship down river. Eli Gritts worked there for a while. I guess it was him tipped them off about the workers' payroll. Or maybe Flinn and Gilpatrick were out for vengeance on me.'

'So what happened?'

'I was out of town collecting taxes. Maybe they waited, watched me go. Whatever, when I got back they'd hit the town like a tornado, taken the tobacco payroll, robbed the bank. My townspeople are pretty peaceful. They ain't gunslingers. But apparently two tried to stop them. Henry Smith, the butcher, was shot down in the street. A bank teller, Sam Stevens, was locked in a safe vault and suffocated to death. They were both black men.'

Sheriff Brady gave a whistle of awe. 'Nasty! You reckon they passed this way?'

'Yup. I figure they're heading up river into the Cherokee Strip.'

'So, they must be the ones who raped and killed Eunice Thark. She musta bumped into 'em as she rode her buggy home.'

'That thought had crossed my mind.'

Sheriff Brick Brady cut a slice from a plug of tobacco and popped it into his mouth, starting to chew as he considered this. 'I got bad news for you, McGee. I been to see the town judge. Carol Lindeman has persuaded him that you're the one to go on trial. You're due up in the morning.'

'But' – the black sheriff's eyes glinted with apprehension as he pushed the tray away – 'that's crazy.'

'Crazy or not, it looks like you're for the high jump. The judge has more or less instructed me to start getting a gallows ready and to send for your friend the hangman.'

'George Maledon? He'll tell 'em. He won't hang me.'

'George will have to do what he's paid to do.'

'This is a set-up. You know that, Brady. If anything, I should be returned to Forth Smith.'

'Maybe, but these folks are determined to hang somebody. And you've been elected. They ain't got time for all that due process.'

'Yeah?' It was getting dusk outside, the shadows lengthening, and Otis McGee jumped nervously to his feet as he heard a disturbance outside. He peered through the broken window and saw men gathered in the street, tar flares in their hands. An ornate hearse, drawn by two black horses, with doffing black ostrich plumes, was creaking by and the men and women with the flares followed in procession out to the graveyard. 'It looks like Eunice's funeral. An' I got a feelin' those people will be back and angry enough to carry out their threat to burn this jailhouse down.'

'Carol Lindeman's out at his camp. He ain't gonna help us.' Sheriff Brady looked as nervous as Otis. 'To tell the truth I ain't sure why he butted in this morning 'cept he'd like to see you strung up nice and legal. Well, more or less legal. I ain't in agreement with all this.'

Brady took two boxes of cartridges from his desk and stuffed them into a pair of saddlebags. He reached for his Spencer carbine. 'We ain't got much time.'

'What you mean, Sheriff?'

'I mean we're going after those *hombres* who killed Eunice. The ones you were after. The Flinn gang. They did this, I'm sure of that. It's up to me to go with you and help track 'em down.'

'Sheriff, you're a brick.' Otis grinned widely. 'Is that why they call you that?'

'You called me a fat, lazy bastard.' Brady unlocked the cell door, handed Otis his Colt Frontier. 'I got two horses outside.'

'I left my saddle back down the trail.'

'Yes, I found it, near your dead horse. Your carbine, too. I brought it in. We're saddled up and ready to go. Come on.'

'Why you doing this, Brady?'

'Because I want you to say you've changed your mind about me. Hang on. I'll just leave a note for my deputy.'

He scribbled in pencil on paper: 'Gone after Eunice Thark's killers. Watch the store.'

He carefully unlocked and eased out of the front door, looking about him. It was dark by now and moths were fluttering about the hurricane lamps. Across the street the saloon was lit up but everything appeared quiet. 'Okay,' Brady hissed. 'It's clear.'

But as Otis McGee stepped from the jailhouse, pulling his black preacher's hat down over his brow, a shout rang out. 'The black's gettin' away! Quick, stop him!'

A shot barked out and a slug whistled past Otis's head, splintering into the woodwork. He ducked down, his Frontier in his hand, as three men tumbled from the saloon, guns in their hands, and began blamming away at him. Instinctively, Otis replied, but aimed to maim, or deter, rather than kill. Two of the miners jumped for cover behind a water butt. But the third, the big bearded man, ran across towards them, firing some more. Otis was tempted to put him down, but he backed away, and dodged around to the back of the jail.

Sheriff Brady was already in the saddle. Otis vaulted onto the spare mustang, tucked his Frontier into his shoulder holster and drew his Creedmore carbine from the saddle-boot. He tossed it into the air and caught it by the barrel, whirling his horse around and charging out the way he had come. The big miner came running into the alleyway, raising a rifle at him. Otis swung his carbine and clouted him across the jaw, felling him, as he galloped past. At breakneck speed he went charging down the street, followed by Brady, as the men behind the water butt sent bullets buzzing like bees about their heads. As they raced out of town the long-legged, liver-coloured hound-dog set off after them, barking excitedly.

When they drew their horses in at the riverside, a mile out of town, the dog came gallumping up in great bounds, panting and tail-wagging. 'What in hell's he followin' us fer?' Otis asked.

Brady shrugged and spat a gob of baccy juice to land on the hound's head. 'He seems to have taken a fancy to ya,' he said.

'Go on. Scat!' Otis yelled, waving his carbine at the dog. He spurred his mustang and plunged him into the river, swimming through the deep currents for the far side. Brady laughed when he reached him for the hound was scrambling up the bank, shaking drops from his coat in the moonlight. 'He seems to think he's coming along.'

'Well, he better have another think,' Otis said, and headed away through the shadowy trees. 'We got time to make up.'

Three

Indian Territory, or the Nations, as this large tract of land was otherwise known, was a place of lakes and waterfalls, winding steams and rivers, mountains and forests teeming with game, and wide, windy prairie. It had originally been set aside as the homeland of the "five civilized tribes", the Cherokee, Choctaw, Chickasaw, Creek and Seminole, with their independent tribal governments, a system which worked well up until the Civil War. But after the war it became a dumping ground for defeated Indians, those that hadn't been blown to smithereens by the army's howitzers; sixty-seven different tribes transported there from all over the country. As well as the 12,000 freedmen blacks of the five civilized tribes, other former slaves arrived to establish their own communities like Tatums, Tullahassee, North Fork Coloured, Red Bird and Wild Cat. But the Nations had also become a magnet for outlaws on the lam from white justice, or southern guerillas and drifters, who had grown used to living by the gun. It became renowned for lawlessness in spite of the efforts of brave US marshals to tame the badmen. More recently, on 22 April 1889, the biggest land run in history had been held when the unassigned lands were opened to white settlers and 50,000 raced by buggy, wagon, on horseback or foot to stake a claim. Oklahoma Territory had been born.

Indian Territory had been reduced by more than half to its eastern sector, but there were men like Carol Lindeman who jealously eyed the Indians' remaining land.

He was particularly interested in the land held by the Osage tribe, for his drillings had shown him that it was rich in minerals, mainly oil. Lindeman's family had emigrated to the States from Czechoslovakia and settled in New York. But he had heeded the cry, 'Go West, young man!' and had taken part in the first land run, had prospered by sub-dividing and selling his land, had bought-up some bankrupt rolling stock and formed his own small railroad company. He had headed his track south from the Kansas border into Indian Territory until he reached the Arkansas River and the little town of Tulsa. He had mined for coal, bringing in fellow Slavs to work at coolie wages, and made a good profit sending the coal north. He set up his headquarters in a former ranch house some miles out of town, and paid court to the local school-teacher, Eunice Thark, the only white girl of breeding and beauty in the area.

He had seduced her by promise of marriage, and maybe he would have married her, but he had been warned that he was operating illegally, and the federal authorities at Fort Smith were considering closing down his operation.

So, there was nothing for it, but to become an adopted Indian. He rode out into Osage country and made contact with a chief called Tuca Bachahajo. He was invited into the chief's tepee and squatting down explained, while the pipe was passed around, his desire to dig for coal or the black oil on their land. No Indian was interested in working all day down a dark mine. It was crazy white man's business. But when Lindeman offered to pay in gold for the privilege of mining or drilling, Tuca Bachahajo grinned craftily. *He* was not crazy. 'Go ahead,' he said. 'Go wherever you like.' So a contract was made giving Lindeman drilling rights on the entire reservation.

Carol Lindeman considered himself a lucky son-of-a-gun and, as luck had it, he noticed, sitting behind the warriors, a very pretty Indian girl – slim, with long black hair hanging to the middle of her back. She was dressed in beaded white doeskin, with an ornate beaded headband, leggings and moccasins.

It so happened she was the daughter of the chief, her name translating as several variants of Ice Along the River that Melts in Springtime. Carol Lindeman did not hesitate. He proposed to the chief that he should marry the girl. Tuca Bachahajo was impressed that so important a whiteman should want to marry Ice Along the River, even more so when Lindeman offered gold for her hand. He readily agreed and two days after the death of his former fiancée, Lindeman returned to the Osage village and the marriage ceremony took place. There was much dancing and feasting, and the next morning Lindeman took the seventeen-year-old girl back to his ranch-house. He was now a bona fide Indian and nobody could stop him looking for minerals on his own lands. And, to tell the truth, he was quite taken by Ice Along the River, as she appeared to be by him. For so modest a bride she had proved to be extremely passionate and ardent in bed. It was a shame about Eunice, but for Lindeman the future was looking good. He had every reason to believe that fortune would favour him. He was, he believed, one of those who just couldn't go wrong.

Sheriff Otis McGee and Sheriff Brick Brady kept their horses at a hard lope on the south bank of the Arkansas River, swimming them across its subsidiary streams. This was a land of good sparkling water which had earned it the name of Green Country. There were verdant woods in which the shy antelope hid. Brick shot a small doe and slung it across the back of his saddle for supper. They skinned and roasted it over the fire, and after filling their bellies with the succulent flesh, sat leaned against their saddles watching the stars sparkling out in a clear sky. The hound dog, too, had a belly full of meat tossed to him by Otis, and looked content, apart from licking at his paws – sore from a day chasing after the two riders.

Sheriff Brady filled a pipe and watched the whirling, silvery river rushing by. 'You know,' he grunted, 'sometimes this ain't a bad life.'

'It's always a source of amazement to me that folk cain't be satisfied with what they got,' Otis said. 'This land could give 'em all they need. They oughta be able to live content, side by side. But no, they always got to be robbin' and killin', at each other's throats. Or a good many of 'em.'

'The main trouble, as I see it,' Brick replied, tamping his pipe, 'is that folks got the wanderlust. They reckon they'll get richer if they go on over the next hill. They envy what others got. Their kids go off seeking excitement, adventure, instant riches, and end up as hard-boiled killers in some damn gang.'

Otis grinned, his lips curling back over fine white teeth. 'Would ja believe, thass what happened to me? Yeah, I been a bad boy in my time. I rode with a gang for a while.'

'What kinda gang?'

'Rustling cattle, horse-thieving. We raided the herds that came up the Chisholm Trail crossing the Nations. They were headed, as you know, for the Kansas cowtowns. But we figured that some of those cows were rightfully ours for what them damn southerners did to our people. It was an exciting time for a youngster. I'd got a gun and I knew how to use it.'

'You kill anybody?'

'No, but it was a near thang. I wounded a few. Those Texans didn't let us take their cows without a fight. I seen plenty men killed. When I think about it now they were good men jest doin' their jobs. There were black cowboys, too.'

'What happened?'

'Aw, just after one of our raids we ran into a platoon of cavalry outa Fort Gibson. They took us in. We were lucky they didn't hang us all. But when you're in chains and sent down river to the stockade for a coupla years two thangs can happen. Either you harden, vow to take revenge. Or you see the error of your ways.'

'And you decided to go straight?'

'Yep. I'd seen some bad things happen to my friends. But that was the chance we took. What I didn't like was seeing innocent men being gunned down. It ain't right. So I took their side. I could shoot, so the folks at Wild Cat elected me sheriff.'

'That's the way I see it. Somebody's got to protect the sheep against the wolves. Or try to.' Brady grunted as he pulled his blanket around him, and chucked another log on the fire. 'Trouble is there's too many damn wolf-men in this territory.'

'What do you think of Lindeman? How you meet up with him?'

'I was a railroad guard in Kansas and he offered me a job on his line. Then he suggested I kept law and order in Tulsa. So I took the job. I'm not a Slav, or Slovene, or whatever they call 'em, but we get on well. He's brought these other Slavs in to work the mines, pays 'em a pittance, but they seem satisfied. They got their own church, their own customs, hold their feasts and dances. It's like they're settled here now. Carol Lindeman's a very ambitious man. He's one of those who's got the vision to look into the future. He believes the railroad and oil business is gonna make him rich. Not that he confides in me, but that's the impression I get.'

'You think he's straight?'

'You know a straight businessman? They're as devious as a sack of snakes. I ain't a clue what he's thinking. But he's always been straight enough with me. You know, those miners, they ain't bad people. They were badly upset by Eunice's death. She'd done a lot for them and their children. I must say they don't seem fond of you blacks.'

'Aw,' Otis grinned. 'We always git the fuzzy end of the lollipop. We're used to it. Not that we're inclined to take it any more now we're free. You know, there's something about Lindeman don't ring right with me.'

'I don't know why you keep on about Lindeman, boy,' Brady shouted. 'You got a bee in your bonnet about him. He's straight enough. He ain't the first guy to dump his galfriend in order to marry into money. It happens all the time. That's how society's ordered. Plenty men out here have married Indian gals, too. But, in his case, he hopes it's gonna bring him riches.'

'Jest cut out callin' me boy, will ya, Brady? I ain't ya black *boy*. That's a term of abuse where I come from. I don't need patronizing by some white man even if he did git me outa jail.'

'You watch your mouth, McGee. Don't git smart with me. I'd just as soon take you back to Tulsa and let 'em string you high.' Brady glowered across the fire at him and reached for his whiskey bottle. 'I don't take lip from the likes of you.'

Otis patted the Smith and Wesson .44 beneath his coat and grinned, mockingly. 'Yeah, you could try.'

'Don't tempt me, smartass.' Brady waggled a stubby finger, angrily. 'Anyway, you are a boy in my book, aincha? I bet you ain't even twenty.'

'My purty looks are deceptive,' Otis drawled. 'I'se twenty-five.'

'I wouldn't have guessed.'

They sat in affronted silence for a while, Brady simmering down for he had the uneasy feeling the young black would be faster on the draw than him if he ever tried to take him.

'If your pal Lindeman's so straight, how come he tried to set me up for a hanging?' Otis suddenly asked. 'Maybe he thought if somebody like me was made to pay then there be no further awkward questions asked? Folks would soon forget the whole thang?'

'For Chrissakes!' Brady yowled. 'Forget him. It's obvious who murdered Eunice – those boys you're following. You figure we're on the right trail?'

'Yep. You said those tracks led to the river crossing. I've a hunch those boys are up ahead. If I hadn't been sittin' for twelve hours in your pokey I'd have gained on 'em by now.'

'So, where they heading for? One of them outlaw towns?'

'Who knows? They might cut off along the Cimarron. Or they might have crossed back over the Arkansas and headed north for Kansas. They might have caught the damn railroad for all I know. Or they could have gone along the Cherokee Strip to Black Mesa country. Thass where a lot of these outlaws hang out these days. This is wide open country an' it's like searchin' for a needle in a haystack, ain't it?'

Sheriff Brady pondered this as he tucked his Spencer carbine between his knees and settled down to sleep. 'If we do catch up, you reckon we can take 'em in? There's five fast guns against two of us.'

'We can only try,' Otis sighed. 'You better git some shut-eye. I'll take first watch. We need to make an early start. I'll wake ya about two.'

'Yuh, okay,' Brady grunted, taking a last swig from the bottle.' Goodnight . . . er, Otis.'

'Goodnight, Brick, you ole prick. And, by the way, didn't you know whiskey's banned in the Nations? It's me oughta take *you* in.'

Brady sat up, waggling his finger. 'I've warned you about talkin' smart. Anyway, it's only for my own consumption. I ain't peddlin' it.'

'Thass all right, Sheriff,' Otis grinned. 'I'll overlook it this time.'

Four

When they reached the confluence of the Cimarron River, Brick and Otis rode up its south bank for a while until they saw a rickety old ferry driven by mule-power wheel. A man in a floppy-brimmed hat and ragged clothes was sat on the ferry staging sucking at a corncob pipe. 'Howdy,' he called.

'This Colby's ferry?' Brady asked.

'That's me.'

'A party of men passed by this way in the last couple days?' The black sheriff described them: 'An odious, nefarious-looking bunch.'

'They might have.' Colby sat and placidly puffed smoke. 'My memory ain't what it was.'

Sheriff McGee spun him a silver dollar. 'Maybe that'll jog it.'

Colby snatched and slipped it in his pocket. 'It might.'

Otis pulled his Frontier and spun it on his finger, pointing the business-end at Colby's forehead. 'I'd advise you to start talkin' fast.'

'Yeah?' Colby scratched his unshaven jaw and took the corncob from his toothless mouth. 'Now you

42

mention it, there was a gang of smelly varmints here yes'day noon. I took 'em over. They was arguin' and cussin'. Heard 'em say something about Pawnee.'

'Pawnee?' Brady asked. 'What, the tribe?'

'No, the town. When I git ya to the other side, head on west through the hills and across the plain to the south bank of the Arkansas. Ye'll find it with any luck. So that'll be two dollars each fer the crossin'.'

'Your prices pretty steep, ain't they?' Otis scowled, putting the revolver back in his shoulder-holster.

Colby held out a grubby hand. 'Take it or leave it. I gotta feed my mule, ain't I?'

Otis counted out another four dollars and nudged his mustang forward on deck. When Brady was aboard Colby cast off and set the mule to working the paddle wheels on either side, he, himself leaning on a long pole at the rear to steer them out into the currents.

'All this water power,' Brady said, looking out at the fast-flowing river. 'Seems a pity they couldn't harness it in some way.'

'How they gonna do that?'

'I dunno, but I guess they'll think of some way some day. They got all kinda machines these days. Why, I hear they got a buggy that can go along the trail without horses under its own steam. And they say they're hoping one day that men can fly.'

'Yeah?' Otis laughed. 'And so will pigs.'

As they clattered their horses onto the far bank, he asked Colby, 'Those men: one didn't have a bad scratch across his face, by any chance?'

'How should I know? I don't go inspectin' my

customers' faces,' the ferryman hooted. 'I tell you, they looked a bad bunch. You watch out, boys. An' by the way, that's the Pawnee reservation you're heading across an' they ain't so keen on interlopers, so hang onto ya scalps.' Colby cackled with mirth. 'So long, boys.'

'Look at it go!' Carol Lindeman shouted as oil fountained out of their drilling hole, and he raised his hands in jubilation as the black gunge rained down upon him. His immaculate suit was being ruined but what did he care? 'Boys, we're in the money.'

The fog of gas and the stink of oil which drifted over the Twin Forks site on the Osage reservation had a different tang to the dry coal dust that coated his small mining town of Tulsa. But, as Carol Lindeman breathed deeply in, it was like perfume to him. Where there was muck there was money, as the adage had it. He was standing beneath his crow's nest drilling rig, with its wooden platform at the top, which had been built with little benefit of geological survey. It was more of a wildcatter's instinct but it had proved sound.

'We've hit the big time!' he yelled as the gusher exploded out of the depths of the earth and the 'black gold' splattered around him. Lindeman put up his hands in praise to the sky. He would have been glad to bathe in it.

'Right,' he shouted at his foreman ganger. 'Get it capped and piped. We're gonna start taking a hundred barrels a day out of this one.'

Scientists had discovered that the various hydrocarbon components could be broken down and refined for domestic heating, lighting, cooking, with residual fuel, or 'black oils', for furnace burning and enriching town gas supplies for street lighting and so forth. But that was not his job. All he had to do was mine the crude oil and ship it on the railroad back out of this wilderness to the factories and cities of eastern America. Lindeman had a strong and excited sensation that it was in this that his future lay, that this turgid black liquid trickling through his hair, splattering his face, soiling his clothes, would make him a millionaire.

Lindeman wiped his face and hands with a rag, and after giving some last orders to his gang, swung onto his thoroughbred, who was glad to get away from the foul-smelling scene and set off at a fast trot back towards his owner's run-down ranch-house.

'You got that boiler going?' Lindeman called to his black manservant, James. 'I need a bath.'

'Yassuh!' James, who had been with him from back east, replied. 'It near blowed my damn head off when I lit it but the water's roaring hot.'

'Good.' Carol Lindeman was in the process of renovating the ranch-house with all the latest inventions in fine living shipped in on his railroad. 'Woodburners and whale oil lamps are things of the past, James. You stick with me and we'll head into the future.'

His young bride, Ice Along the River, appeared, her buckskins, too, a thing of the past, attired now in a long-skirted dress of rustling blue silk, beneath which she wore white stockings and uncomfortable

high-heeled bootees. Carol had insisted she threw
away her moccasins and beadwork filet and necklet.
If she were to be his wife she should dress like a white
lady. But, somehow, her new look seemed at odds
with her shiny black hair and dark-copper complex-
ion. She had, however, the natural regal bearing of a
chief's daughter.

Ice Along the River looked somewhat surprised by
Lindeman's appearance, usually fastidiously elegant
but covered now by black ooze. 'What's happened?'
she cried, for she had learned basic English at a
missionary soddy school. 'What do they do to you?'

'What's the matter?' Lindeman grinned at her.
'You got the idea I been tarred and feathered? No.
We've struck a big one, baby. You an' me, we're
gonna be rich.'

'Rich? What you mean?'

'We're gonna have everything we can possibly
want. You know what rich means? Land, money, gold,
diamonds, property. I guess your daddy would count
it in ponies. *We* can have our own damn household
cavalry.'

'But, we have this house, land, our own horses.'
Ice Along the River looked genuinely puzzled. 'We
have all we need. Why should we want more?'

'Because it's there. Reach for the stars, honey,
that's my motto. You Injuns never did get it, did you?
That's why you let everybody trample over you, never
got anywhere. You got to have cash in order to rule
this world.' He gesticulated, wildly, at his blackened
face, hair and clothing. 'This oil is the old black
magic. It's gonna keep us in comfort for the rest of

our lives and our children after us.'

'Your bath is ready, sir,' James butted in. 'You look a bit of a mess, if I might say so. You've trampled it into the house.'

'Oh, who cares?' Lindeman brandished his fists with exasperation. 'I'll buy me another house, and another one after that.'

Ice Along the River shrugged, and smiled in a girlish and mischievous way. Everybody knew that white men were crazy in the head, but her husband seemed crazier than most. She would never have dreamed that she would end up marrying such a man and would have to live like a white lady. There was something not quite right about it but she had learned that the Indian had to adapt to survive. So, she attended Lindeman in his bathroom, taking his soiled clothes. 'Shall I wash these?'

'No,' he roared. 'Chuck 'em into the stove. But take the cash outa my pocket first. James'll lay me some clean clothes out on the bed.' He sank down into the hot water of the tub with a blissful sigh and handed her a brush. 'Here, give my back a scrub.'

Ice Along the River had not yet grown accustomed to the strange pallor of her husband's naked skin. She worked dutifully to scrub the oil out of his hair and from his body and, more gently, traced her fingernails along the blue veins in his muscled arms. 'Carol,' she whispered, 'these riches we will have . . . will my father, my people, benefit at all?'

'Of course they will. I'll see he's all right. Haven't we signed a contract?'

'Yes, but, that was before. It was not for very much.

It was only for a few dollars a month to lease the land. My father did not know that our land would make you rich.'

'You're cuter than I gave you credit for!' Lindeman stuck a cheroot in his mouth as James lit him up, and he lay back. 'What did they teach you in that soddy school? High finance?'

'The missionary lady, Miss Eckerman, she say I learn well, I should go on to a white ladies' college in the east. But' – the slim girl made a grimace – 'I did not want to leave my people.'

'Maybe I'll give you a job taking care of the books. Keep it in the family, eh, gal? Don't worry, I'm an Injun now, ain't I? I'm not going to forget my family, am I?'

'I hope not,' she smiled. 'It is Osage land, after all.'

'No, it's mine by treaty, or, at least, what's under it is. You better believe me. All that oil's legally mine.'

Ice Along the River frowned. 'Yours?'

'Yeah, it's me's put in the capital, the investment, made the discovery. What have you damn Injuns done except sit on your backsides?'

'We?' The girl looked nonplussed as she ceased stroking his body. 'You are like all the white people. You despise us. I thought you were different. You don't care about us.'

'Aw, come on, honey. It's not like that. You, your father, you'll get what's coming to you. But you can't expect to hog the whole caboodle. You must see that I come first. You're with me now, not them.' He reached out for her hand, drew it down into the bath water. 'Come on, honey, do that again. That was nice.'

Ice Along the River frowned, her eyes troubled, but as she was about to resume her caresses there was the thudding of horses' hooves outside and the clatter of spurs, men's rough voices as three of Lindeman's hard men burst into the ranch house.

'It's Vince and the boys,' James called.

'Show Vince in.' Lindeman lay in the warm suds and scowled up as the lanky gunslinger, Vince Hope, in a low-crowned stetson, and a gunbelt slung around his hips, strolled into the bathroom. 'Well, did you get 'em?'

'Nope.' The sullen-faced Hope struck a match and lit a cheroot, sucking in the smoke. 'We took a small posse and followed 'em as far as the Cimarron. But they're gawn across and on into Pawnee territory.'

'So, why have you come back empty-handed? Why are you wasting time? Why didn't you follow?'

'Well,' Hope growled, letting the smoke trickle from his thin lips, 'the posse had had enough. They're only townsfolk. They weren't prepared for a long haul.'

'But there were still three of you. Two of them. Were you scared of them?'

'No, course not. But' – Vince eyed the Indian girl in her fancy dress hanging around his employer's neck and gave a snort of contempt – 'it's all right for you to say that. We were a long way out. How the hell we know where they're headed to?'

'It was your job to follow, to find out. Hand me my robe, James.' Lindeman rose from the tub, his muscular physique and hair-matted chest dripping water as he stepped into a towel, and his wife began dutifully drying him. 'I paid that lump-of-lard sheriff good money to run Tulsa town the way I told him to. Why'd he run off with that black rapist for? I want my fiancée's memory avenged. I want them both dead.'

'Sure.' Vince Hope put a boot heel up on a stool, his eyes contemptuous as he studied them. 'It's all very well for you, Lindeman, to be lounging around here in your hot bath with your li'l squaw, but we're the ones have to go out and do your dirty work. It ain't as easy as it looks. Maybe you should put a bit more cash up front. I got expenses to cover. I'm risking my life. And I need a couple more of the boys as back-up.'

'Don't you come here making your demands of me.' Lindeman raised a hand, pointing threateningly. 'You jumped up gutter trash. What you think I am, made of money? You get a bonus when the job's done.'

'I want one 'fore I start agin.' Hope slapped his revolver butt and flicked his cheroot end into the bath. 'Don't you go callin' me names. You won't find a better shootist than me. What the hell's so important about catching them two, anyhow? They've gawn well away from here. So, I say, let 'em go.'

'You're more of a fool than I took you for, Vince. Them two are lawmen. I don't like lawmen. I don't like anybody nosing into my affairs. Before you know it, unless we get this matter quietly resolved, they'll be dispatching some US marshal from Forth Smith to see what's going on. The federal authorities are the last people I want to take an interest in us. Now do you understand?'

'Yeah, I guess.'

'Come into my office. I'll see what I can afford. Like I was just telling Ice here, I got most my capital tied up in rolling stock and in my mining operations, but let's see.' He led Vince into his office and operated a combination lock on a big iron safe. He slid out a cashbox and removed two bundles of greenbacks. He counted out five hundred dollars onto his desk. 'There y'are, Vince. Another five hundred when the job's done.'

'How about Hank and Reno. This'll do me.'

'You gunmen are real greedy bastards.' Lindeman sighed and counted out two more piles. 'Two hundred each. Okay?'

'Yep.' Vince pocketed the cash. 'Killing don't come cheap, Mr Lindeman. We're professionals.'

'In that case you'll be aware we got to keep this hush-hush. If anyone asks, the black fella – what's his name? – Otis McGee, bribed Sheriff Brady to help him break out of jail. Most likely that's the truth, anyhow. You and your posse go after 'em and shoot 'em down when they resist arrest. Got it?'

'That's how it's gonna be, boss.'

'Right, you can take Slim and Arthur. Logan had better hang around in case there's trouble here. Don't come back until you got better news for me.'

Ice Along the River was listening, concern glistening in her dark eyes. 'Why you want to kill this black man, Carol?'

'Because he raped and killed the white gal I knew before you, that's why.'

'Are you sure he did this? Shouldn't he be given a fair trial? Under the law of the Nations non-Indian fugitives must be taken back to Fort Smith for trial by the federal judge.'

'That ain't how it always happens, honey. Don't you worry your pretty head.' Lindeman hugged the girl to him. 'This is no concern of yours. Like I was just telling Vince, we don't want no busybodies poking their nose into our affairs. Us Indians' – he grinned and winked at the gunman – 'we've never had a fair deal, but I'm gonna make sure we get one. We may be the only minority in the USA with no rights, no freedom, no vote, but there's one good thing – we don't pay federal taxes, neither. And that's the way it's got to stay. We don't want them blood-sucking taxmen getting their teeth into us. They get wind of this they'll be flocking around here in droves like locusts. They never let go.'

'Gee, boss, you sure got a devious mind,' Vince smiled. 'That's one thing that's never occurred to me that it might pay to be an Injun.'

'Well, I doubt if you pay tax on *your* earnings, Vince,' Lindeman said, seeing him out. 'But us businessmen have to look after our interests.'

'I've laid out your tweed suit, suh,' James said, as Lindeman closed the front door. 'And fresh linen.'

'Good. You see that dinner's ready in an hour, James. Me and my wife are going to have a little lay down.' He took Ice Along the River's hand. 'Come on, honey. We got bedroom business.'

*

Sheriff McGee and Brady had reached a dusty white trail across the prairie, first blazed by Nathan Boone in 1843, and were riding their broncs along it at a fast lick when they heard an ululating cry and saw a band of Pawnee appear over a rise in the prairie. A rifle shot cracked out, the bullet whistling past Otis's curly head.

'Hail!' he cried. 'I thought the Pawnees were pacified.'

'It looks from their paint,' Brady shouted, 'that this lot are on the warpath.'

The two men didn't need any further urging but put spurs to their mounts as the Pawnee warriors, in feathers and paint, came swooping down from the hill, screaming and shouting to spine-chilling effect.

'They're trying to cut us off!' Otis yelled, turning in the saddle to glance back at the Pawnee horde galloping across the plain towards them. He could see the sun glinting on the blades of lances and tomahawks and felt the hair of his scalp prickle. 'They look kinda upset about somethang.'

'Head for that stand of blackjack trees,' Brady shouted, veering his horse off the trail.

Otis followed, hanging low over his mustang's neck, eating Brady's dust. The mustang's eyes were bulging with fear, his ears laid back listening to the blood-curling screams behind them and he didn't need any encouragement to flee. Hooves pounding the sunbaked grass he galloped in an arrow-straight line towards the trees. For the moment they were leading this race, but it wasn't a pace they could keep up for long.

When they reached the small wood they pulled their carbines free, leaped from their broncs, and slithered into the undergrowth. Otis crouched behind a bole, aimed his Creedmore, and took out the pony of the leading warrior. Knees caving, it ploughed into the earth, sending two other ponies tumbling with it. It served to disperse the charge, the Indians screaming their anger, but riding away to surround them. Two of the felled riders had rolled clear and were attempting to pull their struggling paints to their feet. They were dressed in buckskins, with feathers entwined in the topknot roaches of otherwise shaven skulls. White and yellow paint smeared their faces. Brady was taking a bead on one of them.

'Wait!' Otis reached out to knock his carbine up and the shot went wild. 'We start killin' and we ain't got a chance. They got us surrounded. I reckon they're already creeping in round the back of us.'

He peered back through the dense foliage of the small wood, half-expecting to see a Pawnee charging at him. He kept his head down as arrows and bullets hissed about him. But the Indians were keeping their distance. They had learned the hard way in the past about white men's modern repeating rifles. Most of them only had ancient longarms, or primitive bows. However, as a lance thudded into his tree Otis realized that such instruments could be extremely effective. He kneeled, loosing off some shots, but aiming more to wing, rather than to kill. One young buck, who came racing up towards them, dropped his raised lance as Otis's slug sliced through his forearm. The boy clutched at the spouting blood and turned back.

The warrior whose pony Otis had killed, was lying on his back a short distance from them, apparently unconscious. But he suddenly stirred and sat up, rubbing his shaven head. His bronze chest was bare but daubed with paint and there was wampum around his neck. 'Hey!' Otis shouted, levering a bullet into the Creedmore's breech and aiming point-blank at the warrior. 'What's your problem?'

The warrior's dark eyes met those of the young black man with menace, suddenly filling with comprehension that he was about to meet his end. Or more than likely. Otis had him at his mercy. 'Why you chasin' us, man? We ain't done nuthin' to you.'

'No,' Brady shouted, pointing to the tin star on his own shirt. 'We're both lawmen. We're on the trail of five badmen. Go tell that to your chief.' He ducked as an arrow hissed past his ear. 'Go on! Before we start shootin' for real. We don't want to kill you. Our mission is peace.'

The warrior stared at them, dully, as if not understanding. He carefully got to his feet, backed away and hurried off to join the howling mob, who were milling about. They saw him run up to an older man with a headdress of eagle feathers trailing down his back, turning to point at them.

The old chief raised his rifle and called out to his warriors, who gradually ceased their shooting and gathered about him. The chief rode forward alone, raising his right hand in a peace sign. He halted his painted pony thirty paces away. 'What are you doing in our land?' he asked.

'We're here after five criminals who have been killing and robbing in my town,' Otis replied, thumbing his chest. 'We had an idea they came this way.'

The chief, like many Pawnee, was fluent in English, and asked, 'Was one of these robbers black?'

'That's right, a young un,' Otis said. 'There's two white trash, a full-blood Cherokee and a breed.'

'We thought you are the black one. This is why we attack you. You say you have nothing to do with these men?'

'The only business we got with them is to take 'em back for their hanging. Why, what they done to you?'

'One of the young maidens from our village was out with her brother collecting herbs and hunting. Those men happened upon her, took her purity, ravished her. They killed her brother when he tried to intervene. They left her for dead, but she lived long enough to describe to us these men.'

'That seems to be their trademark,' Brady growled, lowering his carbine and getting to his feet. 'They ain't men, they're monsters. I'm sorry to hear this, Chief. We're after 'em for more or less the same sort of thing.'

The chief, his dark face gouged by weather and time, gazed at them, solemnly. 'Which way you come?'

'From the Cimarron,' Brady said. 'They ain't back that away. They must be up ahead.'

'You come,' the chief said, beckoning them. 'You come my village.'

The rest of the Pawnees gathered around them, threateningly, weapons raised, jostling and grimacing, until the old chief called out and they parted to let them through. 'My people are very angry,' he said.

'I don't blame 'em,' Otis muttered. 'So are mine.' He spotted the warrior whose pony he had killed, seated now riding double behind another warrior. 'I'm sorry about your bronc, pal. It was the only way of stopping y'all.'

The bare-chested brave scowled and shrugged. 'I owe you a life,' he said.

'Yeah, I guess we coulda killed quite a few of you,' Brady put in, 'but you'd have got us in the end. The black sheriff here acted pretty cool and avoided that.'

'Yuh,' the chief nodded. 'That is good.'

An hour's riding across the gentle undulations of the prairie brought them to the Pawnees' village, which looked like a cluster of earth mounds set each side of a stream. Women in buckskins came running forward angrily, believing them to be two of the offenders. They would have shown no mercy if they were. They had knives in their hands and looked ready to drag them from their horses and hack them to death. But they calmed down when the position was explained. The chief invited them to dismount, leading them into the doorway of one of the larger mounds.

It was dark and cool and remarkably spacious inside, the roof held up by ancient cedar poles over an oval auditorium surrounded by rows of raised seats carved into the earth. An oil flare flickered eerily, and Otis reflected that in the old days, not so long ago, the Pawnee would have sacrificed one of their prettiest maidens at harvest time as tribute to the Morning Star. They had been one of the first tribes out on the frontier to befriend the whites, and had been decimated by disease for their pains. They had voluntarily given up human sacrifice when it was explained that it was not a Christian thing to do.

'Well, I can certainly see why them thugs were tempted to misbehave,' Otis muttered, as a lissom, bare-breasted young girl, in summer wear of only moccasins and a skimpy skirt, brought forward a gourd of drink and offered it him. It tasted like a sweet beer. 'Very nice,' he drawled, grinning at her lecherously.

'Keep your eyes off her, boy,' Brick Brady growled. 'That's what this trouble's all about.'

The girl was smiling and pointing to Otis's hair. 'Sure, go ahead and feel it if you want,' Otis smiled, bowing down and letting her run her fingers through his crinkly mop of tight curls.

'She asks if you are one of the buffalo soldiers?' the chief said.

'So named because they got hair like buff's hide,' Brady laughed. 'She seems to have taken a fancy to you, Otis. Why doncha marry her?'

'Yeah, this might be not such a bad way of living,' Otis replied, as he accepted a bowl containing a mess of meat. 'I only hope this ain't dawg.'

'Eat!' an older squaw ordered, her ample proportions covered by a buckskin dress. 'It bird on water.'

'She means duck,' Brady said.

'Yeah, well she mighta taken the innards out first.'

'Good.' The squaw dipped her forefinger in and

lifted a length of intestine to his mouth. 'Good. Eat!'

Otis rolled the whites of his eyes with revulsion, looking around, but the eyes of the chief and the other seated braves were on him, expectantly.

'You gotta make an effort, Otis,' Brady said. 'They're gonna be offended if you don't.'

'Aw!' Otis reluctantly took the end of the intestine in his mouth and began to nibble. It was evil-tasting and as tough as rubber. He tried to bite a bit off, chomping on it with his strong white teeth, but it wouldn't give. To his horror he saw that the fat squaw, with her bulging chins and breasts, had started on the other end, chewing away, swallowing the intestine down, her wide eyes fixed on his. 'Ugh!' he grunted, almost heaving up.

'Go on, Otis. You gotta meet her halfway. It's their custom of friendship. You can't stop now.'

Otis's cheeks bulged, but he gamely went on forcing himself to swallow. The woman's ugly face was rapidly getting closer and closer as she chewed. Transfixed, he chewed on until they were eyeball to eyeball, noses touching. What happens now? he wondered.

Suddenly the young girl appeared, a thin blade in her hand. She flicked it up, deftly cutting through the gristle, and they fell apart as the warriors laughed. Otis gulped the last bit of gut down, and gripped the older woman's and the young girl's hands, squeezing and raising them in victory sign.

Everybody seemed well pleased, and when they had eaten, a stone pipe was passed around. One suck at this had the effect of making the black sheriff even queasier than he had felt before. 'What you got in this thang?' he asked, his head spinning. 'The happy weed?'

The Pawnee had decided to make a celebration of it, the pipe and beer going the rounds, some of the warriors getting up to do a shuffling dance in the centre of the floor, a drum pounding monotonously, the women, children and men who were watching, joining in a trancelike chant.

'How we gonna git outa here?' Otis asked, somewhat nervously, for the Osage maiden had come to sit beside him and was twining her fingers into his. 'We been here a coupla hours.'

All this talk about blood sacrifice and killing had made him kind of nervous. Some of the heavy-built braves were giving him leery looks as he smiled at the Indian girl and tried to make polite talk. 'What's your name, honey?'

'Espowes,' she said, sweetly, and explained with hand signals. 'Light in the Mountain.' Like the fat squaw, this young nubile one had appeared to have taken a strong fancy to him. Apparently, it was normal for unmarried girls to wander around half-naked. Otis could not help glancing, lasciviously, at the upturned nipples of her petite breasts and her slim body. 'My father, Wound-in-Head, is killed by white man. My mother, Pennahwenonmi you eat with. That means you want me. We live alone. We need man.'

'Yuh? Is that so?' Otis's Adam's apple gave a lurch. What was this: a hustle? 'I ain't in the marriage mart right now, babe. I mean, you're real cute, but I'm kinda busy. I'd love to dally' – he restrained his hands from touching her lissom body – 'but me and my pal, we're a coupla dillies. I mean we gotta go.'

Suddenly the chief, whose name, translated, was Dry Land Crane, clambered arthritically to his feet, and resplendent in his tribal headdress, raised his arms for silence. 'White man and black man,' he intoned, 'we welcome you here as our brothers. Now you must go on your way in pursuit of our enemies. We wish you good fortune. Our spirit is with you. We send twelve of our best trackers to go with you. All we ask is the hair of these men who have offended our people. For this I give to you' – he pointed at Brady – 'my best horse, a gift from the neighbouring Nez Percé people.'

He clapped his hands and a magnificent Appaloosa was led in. One of the world's oldest breeds, the grey, black-spotted horse was the favoured war and hunting mount of the Nez Percé when they had lived in their own northern lands.

Dry Land Crane pointed to the dappled coat and said, 'They are like the snowflakes, no two Appaloosa coat patterns are alike.'

'Thass mighty kinda you, Chief,' Brady muttered, getting to his feet and taking the reins. 'This must mean a lot to you.'

'As much as my granddaughter, Light in the Mountain, means to me. She will be yours' – he pointed to Otis McGee – 'when you return with the scalps of the criminals.'

'Yeah?' Otis saw the bare-breasted nymphet watching, anxiously, and gave her a reassuring grin. 'That's mighty nice.'

Their dozen bodyguards were already swarming about them, and they were escorted out of the gloomy chamber into the light of the setting sun, feeling a trifle unsteady on their feet. The warriors were giving howls and springing onto their painted ponies.

The corpulent Brady was looking with alarm at the feisty Appaloosa. 'Hail,' he said, 'she ain't fer me. I prefer my steady old bay. You want her, Otis?'

'Yeah, exchange is no robbery. You can come back and claim the gal!'

Five

'Well, whadda ya know!' They had not gone a mile from the Pawnee camp when they heard an excited baying and the long-legged liver-coloured hound came lolloping out of some trees towards them. 'In the heat of the fighting I forgot all about that dang thang,' Otis smiled. 'He musta been searching for us. He looks about done in.'

He jumped from his horse and the dog leaped into his arms, panting, licking and tail-wagging, furiously. 'Here y'are, boy.' He lifted him up and laid him across the Appaloosa in front of his saddle horn, swinging back aboard. 'You gonna ride in style.'

'What you doing?' Brady asked. 'You gone *loco*? I thought you wanted to be rid of that durn coonhound?'

'Aw, we can't leave him here,' Otis grinned. 'He might get ate.'

'Come on, let's git.' Brick Brady set his horse after the party of Pawnee scouts, who were galloping away into the sunset.

'Hold tight, fella,' Otis said, and spurred his new

horse in pursuit. 'It's true, I musta gone soft in the head.'

When darkness closed in, they hunkered down among the half-naked Indians squatted around a small fire, who were jabbering in their own tongue. Brady crushed coffee beans with his carbine butt, boiled up a thick brew in his canteen and passed it, and his tobacco, around. He leaned back against the saddle as their horses grazed and said, 'That pretty li'l Indian maiden, the one who had your eyes popping out on stalks, she would probably have been the chosen one in the old days. All summer she would be treated like a princess, and, when the harvest came, she would have been dressed in finery and carried around on a palanquin. She would have been ritually sacrificed to the gods to make the rains come again and the plants grow, and skinned—'

'Skinned?'

'Yeah. The priest would have put on her skin to dance about to show she was reborn.'

'It musta been a tight fit.'

'Yeah, that li'l gal don't know how lucky she is. The great chief Petalashero agreed to stop the practice back in 1818. Nowadays they make do with sacrificing an antelope and wearing his hide.'

Otis peered about him at the warriors in their paint and shaved-headed finery. 'They sure are a weird bunch. It's like they come from a different world.'

'Yeah, a world in a different time warp, ten thousand years before this modern one. Somehow they got passed by.'

When the moon rose high, they saddled-up, and headed on again, but the dawn revealed just rolling prairie, no sign of the fugitives they were seeking. They jogged on their way most of the day until they reached the small township of Pawnee and the reservation agency cabin and store. A lanky scarecrow of a man, in Quaker hat and black suit, not dissimilar to that Otis wore, came out and shouted, 'What in Sam Hill's going on? What these boys doing in warpaint?'

Sheriff Brady explained the situation, that an Indian maiden had been dishonoured and murdered, along with her brother, and they were after vengeance. 'They nearly took our scalps by mistake,' he said, taking off his hat to wipe the sweat from his gleaming bald dome. 'Only they wouldn't have had much use for mine.'

'We're on the trail of the Flinn gang, escaped felons, robbers and murderers, mixed race, five of 'em – white, black, Cherokee and breed,' Otis put in. 'You seen 'em?'

'Well, yes,' the agent, called Rafferty, replied. 'They stayed here last night. I sold them flour and jerked beef and fresh horses. They seemed to have plenty of cash.'

'You allowed to do that?' Otis asked. 'Sell the Indians' provisions?'

'We turn no one from our door,' Rafferty piously replied.

'No, not if they got stolen cash to spend and line your pockets.'

'Just what are you insinuating, you black—'

'Hold it with them words,' Brady snapped. 'Before

you turn nasty, mister, this here's a lawfully elected sheriff of a black township.'

'He's got no jurisdiction here,' Rafferty muttered, sourly. 'How was I to know who they were? I gave them supper at my table and they bedded down in the stable.'

'You were lucky they didn't cut your throat and take everything you got,' Brady remarked, stepping down to water his bronc at the wooden horse trough.

'I thought they were reluctant to join us at worship,' Rafferty replied, and turned to address the warriors. 'You boys better git that paint wiped from your faces, and go back to your village. You're not allowed to take the law into your own hands any more, or go any further. Or are you looking for a spell in the guardhouse?'

A couple of Indian police, in their straight-brimmed hats and dark uniformed jackets over cotton pants, had appeared, with carbines in their hands, and began shouting undoubtedly similar instructions at the mounted Pawnees. The warriors replied, spiritedly, brandishing their weapons, but soon became browbeaten and sullen. It was obvious they were losing the argument.

'Tell 'em not to worry,' Otis called. 'We'll catch up with them varmints.'

They watched the Pawnees dejectedly turn tail and amble their ponies away until they were just a cloud of dust on the prairie. 'Poor devils, they're like dogs with pulled teeth these days,' Otis muttered. 'They've had all the fight knocked out of them.'

Pawnee town was just a collection of shanties on

the prairie, no different to many white settlements, with men, women and children going about their business, loading or unloading their wagons at the agency store, or sitting in the shade beneath a stars-and-stripes hanging limply from a flagpole – except they were all Pawnees, some in white folks' garb. There was a livery, forge, corrals, grain silo, clothing emporium . . . but no saloon or gunshop.

Otis and Brady made a few purchases – coffee and green beans, a sack of splitcorn for their broncs, tobacco for the white sheriff, a bag of bulls-eyes for the black one – whistled to the dog, and made a beeline north across the plain the way the outlaws had gone.

When they reached the wide Arkansas river they swam their horses across and made camp on the north bank as night set in. 'Where you figure they're aimin' for?' Otis asked, as he stamped his boot to break up dry kindling. Brady was knelt over the fire, stirring at the pot.

'Looks to me like they're heading for Pawhuska town, the capital of the Osage Nation. It's on a big lake, coupla days ride ahead. They could be planning to cross the Verdigris and reach the Cherokee Strip. Or, who knows, I got a funny gut feeling they might follow the Verdigris back down towards Catoosa or Tulsa.'

'You mean we could be going in a circle?' Otis exclaimed. 'On some wild goose chase?'

'Could be. Catoosa's a wide open town, a magnet for every cheap cattle thief or scumbag seeking refuge in the Nations. It's a real hellhole.'

'Jeez!' Otis hurled a log out towards some beavers busily paddling about their lodge. 'We might just as well have sat and waited for 'em to come back to us instead of traipsing halfway round the Territory.'

'It's only a hunch,' Brady muttered. 'They could be anywhere.'

'Hell take Carol Lindeman,' Vince Hope yelled, as he and his five gunmen rode into Catoosa. 'Why's he got a bee in his bonnet about Brady and that black for? They ain't likely to hang around with a lynch party on their heels. They'll be well outa the Territory by now. I ain't wastin' my time chasin' after 'em. We'll hang around here, burn his cash, paint the town red for bit, then go back, say there's no sign of 'em.'

'*Yahoo!*' The sweaty, grimy, stubbly and fat-gutted Arthur Simms seconded this. 'I cain't wait to git my hands on one of them li'l hoo-rees.'

Catoosa was both railroad town, on Lindeman's line south from Kansas to Tulsa Town, with a rickety wooden bridge built across the Verdigris, and port for those few flat-bottom steamboats and hand-poled rafts still transporting produce down river to meet the Arkansas at Muskogee and on to the army stockade at Fort Gibson.

But mostly, it was a den of iniquity, with bad bootleg liquor and even badder girls available at a price to the criminal fraternity who gathered there. Booze was, of course, banned in the Nations, as was prostitution. The Hanging Judge, Isaac Parker, had appointed 200 deputy marshals to operate from his court further down the Arkansas at Fort Smith in an attempt to bring law and order to the Indian Nations. He had sent to the gallows 88 of those criminals his marshals brought back for justice, but not without a price: sixty of his deputy marshals had been gunned down in their brushes with badmen. Many now fought shy of places like Catoosa, where their chances of staying alive were at a premium, and were inclined to turn a blind eye to the whiskey and 'white slave' traffic. Prohibition only appeared to fan the flames of demand.

So, Vince Hope and his boys were licking their lips in anticipation of a high old time as they went trotting on their horses like a pack of wild dogs seeking prey into the busy streets of Catoosa. Folks about their lawful business scattered as the band of *viciosos* rode roughly through heading for the parlour house of Pearl Starr, daughter of the even more notorious Belle Starr, who had been recently ambushed and shot from her saddle, some said by her son. From being a common prostitute, put 'on the game' by her mother, Pearl now found herself owner of a ranch and two profitable brothels.

Vince, the tubby Arthur, Slim Higgins (renowned for his prowess with the knife), a gangling hulk in greasy buckskins, Hank Martin, and a razor-faced dude, Reno, pulled in their broncs outside two white-washed single cottages knocked into one – known as The Ladies' Academy – hitched their reins to the fence outside and hung on the bell-pull. A slot peep-hole opened and Pearl peered through. 'Yes?'

'Hiya, baby,' Vince grinned. 'Open up. We could

drink the Verdigris dry, if it was whiskey, that is.'

'Whiskey? We don't sell whiskey. Who told you that?'

'Aw, come on, sweetheart. Everybody knows.'

Pearl gave them the once-over, but they did not look like law enforcers. She had been having some hassle of late with the authorities at Fort Smith who had vowed to close her down, and, in particular with the big black Marshal Bass Reeves and his sidekick, Marshal Bill Tilghman. However, that was another story. These five looked fine. The peephole snapped to, and they heard the door being unbolted. 'Come on in, boys,' Pearl smiled, opening up. She ushered them in and quickly slammed shut the door again.

'So, where's the action, honey?' Reno curled an arm around her waist. 'I'm kinda partial to a curvy gal like you.'

'Hang on!' Pearl pulled herself free, a blush of agitation rising to her young, if rather puffy face beneath the powder and paint. Her turquoise silk dress was tightly restraining a plump bosom from bursting fee and she gave it a hitch-up. 'I like my gentleman callers to behave. If you will hand in your hats here, and guns, I'll take you through to the parlour. All my young ladies are high-quality girls, college-educated, of genteel disposition. You are welcome to polite discourse and to dance to the phonograph, the only one in the Territory, I might add. But we frown on coarse language and rough horseplay. Any breakages must be paid for. As to terms, we charge—'

'Aw, cut the crap,' Reno scowled, grabbing her

again. 'We got plenty of cash. You'll do me, babe. Let's do it.'

'Please! How dare you!' Pearl broke away from him again. 'If you can't behave I'm going to have to ask you all to leave. Anyway, I'm not on the menu these days.' She glanced at Reno's sharp eyes like dark thorns in their slits. 'Not unless I want to be, that is.'

'Come on, give the li'l lady a break.' Vince pushed Reno aside. 'Do as she asks. Hand in your guns, boys. What's the harm?'

'Thank you.' Pearl breathed with relief as they clattered iron down and she stowed it behind the reception desk. 'I'm sick of rowdies peppering my ceiling with their six-guns. It's a dangerous sport. Why, I was in bed one day when one parted my legs. A bullet, I mean. It came right up through and out the roof.'

She waggled, in the tight dress with its fashionable bustle, over to an adjoining door and rapped. 'It's me, Pearl.' More bolts were drawn and she beckoned the gunmen through. 'There we are. May I introduce Heather, and Ruby and. . . .'

There were seven young ladies dressed in the height of fashion, seated on plush armchairs or red velvet settees, one reading a leather-bound book of verse, another embroidering a sampler, a skinny one at the far end tinkling at an upright piano.

'Pleased to meet you, gentlemen.' Heather was in a sumptuous dress of blue shimmering shantung, modestly buttoned, with rustling underskirts. She wore a 'curtains' hairstyle, its brown folds falling away from a middle-parting. 'How kind of you to call.'

She spoke in such a cultured manner that the men, in their dusty range clothes, were suddenly tongue-tied; even Reno, awkwardly taking their places beside the girls.

The room was a clutter of exotic Victorian bric-a-brac, heavy chintz curtains, and garish carpets, with an ornate oil lamp burning low. 'Have you come far?' Heather asked, leading some polite chit-chat.

'Yeah.' Arthur gave a guffaw. 'All the way from Tulsa town, but the boss don't know. We're s'posed to be out chasin' a coupla jail-busters.'

'You're not law enforcers?'

'No. More what you'd call a private army,' Vince laughed.

'Well, where's the friggin' whiskey?' Reno asked, irritably.

'Yeah, thass what we're here for,' Slim put in, scratching at his underarms.

'As I was saying,' Pearl smiled, 'our prices are sky high because this is contraband and we're accustomed to dealing with officers and gentlemen. Our clientele is the best. Are you sure you can afford us?'

'Course we can afford you.' Vince dug in his coat pocket and produced a wad of greenbacks. 'There's two hundred there. Just keep us happy, ladies, 'til the money's gone.'

'Ah, that's different.' Pearl snatched up the cash and rippled a finger through it, tucking it quickly away into a purse. 'Perhaps I misjudged you.'

'Yeah.' Marina was a more down-to-earth and dumpy blonde. 'We thought from your stink you was just dumb cowhands.'

'Stop tickling that piano, Josephine, and put a record on,' Pearl cried, going to sit beside a huge Russian samovar. 'Tea, gentlemen?'

'Tea,' Reno sneered. 'We don't want no damn tea.'

Pearl patted her brown curls, gave a dimpled smile and a significant wink. 'This is what you might call special.' She passed a cup and saucer to Vince, who sampled it, little pinky raised.

'Whoo!' he whistled. 'Git a load of this. Nearly blows your durn head off.'

Suddenly, the creaking voice of some European opera singer squeaked from the horn of the record machine as the coloured girl, Josephine, furiously wound the handle. 'Care to dance?' Ruby asked, rising to her feet in her velvet gown and curtseying to Vince. She coiled his arm around her waist and led him back and forth in a Texas two-step.

Others of the girls jumped up and dragged the men into the shindig, bumping and grinding, squealing and giggling as the boys grappled them hard.

'I don't care for dancing,' Heather murmured, taking strong hold of Hank's horny hand and pulled up her dress and frou-frou underskirts to reveal shapely legs in white stockings, peekaboo slippers, and lace pantalettes. She snaked the manicured fingers of her other hand up around his neck, gripping his greasy hair, and pulled his face to her, kissing him with open lips. 'I just love filthy-stinking *hombres* like you, Hank,' she whispered.

'Yuh?' There was a moment of disbelief, but Hank didn't waste any more time, rolling the divinely decadent Heather onto her back on the deep settee like some fevered mongrel.

'More tea?' Pearl asked Reno, refilling his cup, and smiling impishly. 'How about you and me go upstairs? You've won me over.'

Northeast Indian Territory was a land of great scenic beauty, with verdant meadows, tree-girdled lakes, wooded hillsides, deep springs, rushing waterfalls, dogwood trails and meandering rivers; a land where game was plentiful, and farming thrived.

However, Jed Flinn's gang were blind to the beauties of the Osage land's rolling blackjack hills, nor interested in legal profit. They planned to get rich quick at the expense of more honest and hardworking humans. Their method was to hit a town hard and ride on out, and Pawhuska, capital of the Osage nation, was to be no exception.

The Osage had once been a warlike people who preyed on their more peaceful neighbours, the Cherokee, but now they had been persuaded to adapt to 'civilized' ways. So much so that they had built themselves a tribal meeting house of split logs in the small lakeside town where the principle chief, Thomas White Bird, spent much of his time attending to tribal business. He had abandoned the feathered costume of his forefathers for a blue, silk-faced frockcoat, checked trousers, polished boots, and a blue bow tied about the starched collar of his cotton shirt. He had even had his long black hair trimmed shorter, and parted in a whiteman's style. He was sitting at his desk, quill pen in hand, attending to his communal accounts and correspondence on that particular morning when he heard the sound of gunshots from the street outside.

When Thomas White Bird and two of his clerks went to the door of the big cabin they were astounded to see their normally peaceful main street under siege from five gunmen, who were racing their horses back and forth taking shots with revolvers and carbines at the town's four uniformed police, or whosoever else showed themselves. Unarmed citizens, panicked by the flying bullets, were seeking cover, as was an Indian woman, dragging a tearful child, who was running up the path to the tribal cabin. White Bird pulled her into what he believed would be safety as he watched the Osage police valiantly attempting to defend the town. But the ferocity of the hardened gunmen took its toll: one officer, Tuske Ker, was sent tumbling as he took cover behind a horse trough; another, John Buzzard, was shot in the back as he sprinted across the street, their blood spilling into the dust.

Too late, Thomas White Bird remembered the revolver in his desk drawer, for as he turned back into the cabin, ushering the woman and child, and his clerks before him, a thin-faced man, Jed Flinn, leaped his mustang over the picket fence, rode it towards him, a sawn off shotgun aimed at the group in the doorway.

'All right, come on out of there,' Flinn drawled. 'You ain't goin' nowhere.'

'What do you want?' White Bird pleaded, putting out his arms to protect the woman and whimpering child. 'Take me. Spare these others, please.'

Flinn's long, wolfish jaws opened in a vicious grin. 'I'll kill y'all if you don't tell them over there to come on out.'

The two other Indian police had taken refuge in a livery loft across the road where they were giving the gang problems with fast sniper fire – already Charlie Gilpatrick was bleeding from a neck wound. The black man, Eli Gritts, the Cherokee, Blue Duck, and the breed, Tadpole, were being forced to back off and take cover themselves.

'Tell 'em we'll burn this town to the ground and slaughter y'all if they ain't out by the time I count to ten.'

The chief hesitated, but a glance at Flinn, his glinting grey eyes, and the steady aim of the two dark holes of the twelve gauge, persuaded him. He strode down the path to the fence, his hands raised, and shouted up to the officers in the loft, 'It's no good. They are threatening to kill us all. To avoid any more bloodshed it is best you surrender.'

Flinn beckoned the woman and child to precede him and, still on horseback, aiming at their backs, he followed them down the path and bellowed out, 'Toss out your guns or these get it first.'

There was a pause as the men in the loft considered their position, then they slowly showed themselves and pitched their carbines out into the street. One, Cheho Jim, swung out of the loft and lightly jumped down. The other, Spring Frog Moody, lowered himself more carefully from the crane used to haul bags of grain into the loft.

As he hung there, Gilpatrick walked forward and fired his self-cocking Colt Thunderer .45 twice into his chest. Spring Frog twisted like a scalded cat and fell to the ground with a thud. Cheho Jim crouched and whipped out his knife, but was too late. Gilpatrick blasted him from point-blank range, bowling him over, and emptied his cylinder until the men on the ground had ceased all movement.

'One of *them* did this to me,' he growled, by way of explanation, pointing with the smoking barrel at the bloody weal on his neck beneath his pimply young face.

'You, I take it, must be the mayor.' Jed Flinn prodded the sawn-off into the back of White Bird's head.

'I am the principle chief of the Osage,' White Bird replied with defiant dignity. 'You won't get away with this.'

'You Injuns don't have banks, but you keep your communal loot in here, what you call your treasury, so I hear. So you're gonna hand it all over, Chief, every last cent, 'less you wanna go the way them other two went. Or' – he grinned – 'maybe I'll kill the woman and kid first.'

The Cherokee, Blue Duck, in his suit, feather in his high-bowled hat, had joined them. 'Let me kill him. We have blood feud.'

And the Choctaw breed, Theophilus Tadpole, sniggered. 'Yeah, an' I'll have the squaw.'

Thomas White Bird sighed, deeply. 'Just take what you need and go.'

'Lead on, pal,' Flinn drawled, swinging from his horse. 'Boys, cover me. This won't take long.'

In a few minutes he emerged, triumphantly raising in his hand a sack of gold coin taken from the chief's safe. 'How about this?'

'Watch out!' Gilpatrick shouted, pointing to the cabin door.

Thomas White Bird was standing there, a revolver in his hand, arm outstretched, aiming at Flinn. There was an explosion and flash of flame, but the bullet whistled harmlessly over Flinn's head as he ducked aside. The chief did not have time to fire again. Flinn blasted him with both barrels, and he staggered back against the wooden door, a retch of surprise and agony on his face, slowly sliding to the ground, his frock coat and shirt decimated by shot.

'You cain't trust nobody these days,' Flinn sneered, as the gunsmoke curled and drifted about him. He took two cartridges from his pocket and reloaded. 'Right, we got a good haul. Let's go.'

'Ain't we gonna have some fun first?' Theophilus Tadpole's fist was clutching the cowering Indian woman's hair, and waving a revolver in his other hand. 'I'll teach this one how to scream.'

'No, leave her. We ain't got time. I got a feelin' we're being followed.'

'If so,' Gilpatrick suggested, 'why don't we wait for him, or them, whoever it is, and blast 'em to hell?'

Flinn considered this. 'I ain't sure. It's just a hunch. Nah, we'll go. We'll head for Catoosa. There's plenty wimmin there, Tadpole. White wimmin.'

The breed disdainfully threw the squaw aside and went to unhitch his horse, holstering his revolver and mounting up like the others. As one accord they went at a fast lope out of the small town and headed east towards the Verdigris River leaving the Pawhuska citizens to show themselves and examine their dead, wondering what had hit them.

Six

When she removed her straw-bonnet, Violet Thark revealed a crowning glory of chestnut hair, tumbling in waves about her pertly pretty face. Large, upturned eyes about a rather prominent bridge of nose gave her a somewhat startled look, counterbalanced by the wideness of her mouth, the fleshy lower lip imparting a sultry sensualness. She was a big-boned, well-built girl and her sturdy bosom within the pink candy-striped dress trembled and shook to the rocking movement of the locomotive on which she was travelling. Violet might not be classically beautiful but she was certainly a sexually attractive girl and constantly received the attention of men's eyes, and no doubt, lustful thoughts, especially in these wild parts where good-looking white women were few and far between.

'Where ya from, leddy?'

Violent looked even more startled when one of the two trappers sat in the double-seat opposite suddenly addressed her. A scurvy duo in greasy, fringed buckskins, unshaven, with shoulder-length hair, the one who spoke wearing a coonskin cap. She had been attempting to avoid eye-contact since they boarded the train at a halt in the woods hefting their pelts. But she could sense their steady gaze, feel their eyes crawling over her, and wished her bosom would not bounce so. She tried to hold it steady with her arms, and replied, with a brief glance, 'Kansas City.'

'Ya don' say,' the one in the cap with the tail hanging down beside his ear drawled, and continued to watch her steadily. 'Kansas City?'

'Yes.' She returned to peering out of the window, watching the hills and trees and streams tumbling past as the little 'Katie' locomotive, with its tall stack and cow-catcher, rattled its two carriages and baggage car around the curves in the track. Its steam whistle was whoo-whooing away, probably to warn some animal on the line for she had glimpsed antelope in the woods. 'I'm going to Tulsa.'

'Tulsey Town, huh?' Coonskin cap pondered this and spat a gob of brown baccy juice into the aisle. He nudged his silent pal. 'All on your ownsome, girlie?'

'Yes.' Violet did feel very alone. She had been working as a medical assistant in Kansas City when she had received the horrifying news of her sister, Eunice's, death, and its awful implications. She hadn't hesitated to ask for leave of absence, had packed a small bag and taken the Pullman express as far as Wichita. There she had changed to this smaller, slower line, which stopped at every halt along the way. Apparently, it was owned by Carol Lindeman, the man to whom her sister had been engaged, a man she had never met. She wished it would put on speed and get to where it was going. Violet had an uneasy sensation in the pit of her stomach as they crossed the sere, dry prairie of the Cherokee Strip, recently opened to white settlement, and entered the darker and densely wooded country of Indian Territory. She could not get over how wild and lonesome it looked, and the rough-looking characters who clambered aboard did not allay her apprehensions, especially these two, with their ancient, long-barrelled rifles and their pungent packs of skins. She was not sure whose was the worse aroma, the hides or theirs? And the ceaseless spitting? Why did all these western men chew and spit? It was most unhygienic. 'It's just a brief visit,' she said.

'Just a brief visit,' Coonskin repeated, and grinned his gnarled, bearded face at her fancy way of talking, nudging his friend once more. 'How's that?'

'I—' Violet frowned as she faced them. What business, she wanted to ask, was it of theirs? As the train increased speed, clouds of coal smoke rolling past the window, her breasts began bobbing involuntarily again, and she saw the unfeigned fascination in their eyes. 'I'm attending my sister's funeral. No, I'll probably be too late for that. But I want to see she has a decent headstone, and find out what happened.'

Coonskin's eyes brightened. 'Why, what did happen?'

'I don't know. That's what I want to find out. She was murdered, you see.'

'Murdered?' Coonskin sprang upright from his slumped position. 'You hear that, Jake? I don't like the sound of that. We oughta look after this li'l gal. We're gittin' off at Tulsey Town' – he gave it its old name – 'we'll find ya a place to stay. Y'll be all right with us.'

'No,' Violet hurriedly protested. 'That's very kind of you to offer, but I've made arrangements,' she lied, 'by telegraph.'

'No, purty gal, you better come with us.' He pointed a blackened finger at her. 'We got a cabin not far out in the woods. You'll like it thar.' He grinned gappily. 'We don't want another of ya gittin' murdered, do we?'

'Nah.' Jake suddenly cackled. 'You come with us, missy.'

'No, thank you.' Violet wished the train was less crowded and she could find somewhere else to sit. She felt trapped by these trappers and their evil-smelling bundles of skins. She had begun to hate the smoky, dirty, rocking and rolling steam train. Smoke and coal grits wafted through the open windows, and she suddenly caught a stinging grit in her eye. She was blinking, tears rolling, trying to wipe the grip free with her hanky. Suddenly she felt a hand grop-ing her knee, and Coonskin's grinning face was up close. 'Here, let me help ya,' he said, taking the handkerchief, spitting on it, and poking at her eye. 'Open wide.' Violet did so, petrified for several seconds. 'Got it!' he yelled. 'There yar.'

'Thank you,' she breathed, as he backed away. She put her hand to her brow and pretended to sleep. Oh, my God, she thought. Whatever next?

'Uh, uh!' As they rode along the edge of the ice-blue and placid Pawhuska Lake towards the tumble of town, Otis McGee saw the crowd of Indians standing beside a rise on the bank beneath a raised platform of sticks. A chanting and mournful wailing drifted to them on the summer breeze. 'What they caterwaulin' about?'

When they got nearer they could see there were five bodies laid out in robes on the platform and the Indians, many in ceremonial dress, turned angrily to stare at the two intruders.

Brady grunted, 'It looks to me like them bastards have struck again.'

Otis showed his sun-gleaming badge. 'Which way they go?' he shouted.

When one of the Osage pointed to the north-east, Otis cried, 'Right, we're going after 'em.' He turned his Appaloosa in the direction indicated and shouted to Brady, 'We gotta push hard. We ain't gonna waste no more time.'

Jed Flinn and his vari-hued gang had forded the Verdigris River and headed east through a gap in the hills towards Bartlesville, which in a few years time would become the scene of the biggest oilrush of the century, but was presently just a hick farming town. They bypassed it and turned south down the Coney River.

'This should throw anybody followin' off our scent,' Flinn said, as they camped by the riverside. 'Nobody can run down me. I got the instincts of a fox. I fooled 'em into thinkin' we're headin' north-east for the Kansas line. Nobody'll guess we're goin' back south towards Catoosa and Tulsa.'

He had spread his blanket on the ground and was counting out the gold coin into five piles. 'Who'da thought them Injins would have this tucked away in their treasury?'

'Holy Moses, we're rich,' the scrawny Gilpatrick yelled, tipping his share into his saddlebags. 'I cain't wait to spend some of this on liquor and prairie nymphs. An' I'm gonna git me a new gun like yours, Jed.'

'This is the latest model there is, brought out in '87,' Flinn replied, pulling the Smith & Wesson and twirling it on his finger. 'You would have to order one from the factory. The Safety Hammerless double-action, thass what they call it.'

'Yeah, but it's got a hammer,' Charlie pointed.

'Of course it's got a hammer, dimwit. How else could it fire? But it's got a safety lever on the hammer. A child couldn't discharge it. The trigger's got a long, hard pull. You have to go right back. But, try it, Charlie, you'll notice a distinct pause just before you let off the hammer. That's unusual for a self-cocker and gives you time for greater accuracy.'

'That why you're such a good shot?' Charlie said, taking aim at an antlered deer swimming across the river downstream. The report clapped out, the bullet spurting the water by the buck's nose, making him turn and hurriedly swim back.

'Don't waste my ammo,' Jed cried, restraining him. 'I ain't got that much left. But you see what I mean. This is an expensive handgun. Cost me twenty-five dollars.'

'*Whoo!*' Charlie whooped. 'As much as that. I only

paid seven-fifty for this ole Colt.'

'Yeah, he's a genius that Daniel Wesson. This gun's got a range of two hundred and fifty yards. I'm a natural good shot, but this piece surely improves my aim. You may have noticed.'

'Yeah, I sure have.' The young Charlie Gilpatrick had a craven awe of the older man. It was Flinn who had devised the way of busting out of state prison, he who had led them on most of their heists. As leader and lieutenant of the gang, it was Jed and Charlie who did most of the talking, the non-white boys, Wild Duck, Eli and Tadpole, mostly remaining in silence, except for the occasional ribald remark, or grunt of assent. All were now dyed-in-the-wool killers, but none wished to test the notorious hair-spring temper of Flinn. 'The way you took that chief out, too, with your shotgun, that was a sight for sore eyes!'

'The revolver for long range, the sawn-off for short range – that's the way to do it.' Flinn tossed the coins in his palms, before packing his share away in a leather pouch. 'Nine hundred dollars apiece, that ain't a bad haul. You stay with me, boys, and we'll all retire young. I'm going to suck the Nations dry 'fore heading north. I'm gonna buy me a nice ranch up Wyoming way some place, change my name, git me a squaw, and settle down. Nobody'll know who I am.'

'Aw,' Charlie squeaked, 'not me. A ranch is too much dang hard work. Me, I'll buy me a saloon and whorehouse, git drunk and laid every day fer free.'

The others grinned at this idea and ventured a few foul remarks on how they, too, would like to laze their lives away. 'I won't have one squaw,' Wild Duck said. 'I'll have six.'

Flinn cut them short. 'You durn young fools need to invest your cash in something that'll pay. Ranching ain't hard work if you own the whole caboodle. You got cowhands to do the work for ya, ya dumbclucks. I'll git me a big luxurious ranch-house with a whole cellar of whiskey and some li'l serving gals to help while the winter away. I got it all worked out. All we gotta do is a coupla more big jobs, then I'm headin' for Wyoming.'

'Like what?' Charlie asked. 'What we gonna do next, Jed?'

Jed Flinn scratched at his long, stubbled jaw, as he stretched out his long legs, laid back on his saddle, watching the river's flow as the moon rose. 'I dunno. But, ain't I heard that them miners an' oilmen in Tulsa town git paid at the end of the month? A little birdie whispered to me that the cash is brought in on the local from Wichita. It's almost the end of the month, so that should be coming through any day now. It's worth a try.'

'What, rob the durn train?' Eli Gritts asked. 'I ain't never done that before. How we stop it?'

'It's easy black boy,' Flinn grinned. 'I'll show ya how. You just follow me. And if the payroll ain't on the train then we'll rob the damn passengers.'

'OK, whitey,' Eli grinned back. 'I guess you're the boss.'

'Thass enough of your lip. Yeah, we've been on a winning streak, boys, since I took over this gang. I figure we could be lucky again.'

*

Pearl Starr yawned and stretched as she felt the warmth of the man's slim hard body beside her. For moments she wondered who he was, what he was doing there, then turned and saw Reno's hard-hewn, hawklike features, his naked torso with its animal-like matt of hair. 'Hey,' she murmured, 'what you doin' here? We musta had a hard night.' She listened to the birds twittering under the cottage eaves and saw that it was already light. 'Hell, I need a shot.'

Reno put a hand to his throbbing head and groaned, 'Me, too.'

Pearl, in her silk petticoat with blue, flowered embroidery, leaned over to the night table and found a small bottle. She measured out ten good drops into a glass and topped it up with water from a flask. She tipped it back and swallowed it down. 'Ahh,' she sighed.

'What's that? That ain't whiskey.'

'Laudunum,' she said, matter-of-factly. 'The lady's secret pleasure. I need one 'fore I start the day.'

'Laudanum?' Reno scoffed, leaning over to examine the bottle. 'Count me out. What about some coffee?'

Pearl was waiting for the hit. 'Go ask Marina.' She lay back, closing her eyes blissfully as it came, hitting the back of her head and surging down through her body, only vaguely aware of the young, hard-muscled gunman rolling out of bed and, on the landing, bawling, 'Marina, git the coffee on. And bring me some hooch. That's Pearl's orders.'

'Get it yourself,' Marina screeched back, but

relented, 'Aw, all right.' She appeared at her bedroom door in a dressing gown, her blonde hair tangled, looking like she'd been pulled through a hedge backwards. She tottered towards the stairs and groped her way down. 'Won't be long.'

'Who's in there with ya?'

'Arthur. Lump o' lard's snorin' like a friggin' pig.'

'Yeah, I can hear,' Reno said, and went back to Pearl, climbing into bed with her. 'What's that stuff do for you?'

'Makes me feel good,' she murmured. 'Thassall.'

'Well, it ain't no good for you, I can tell you that.'

'Don't lecture me, honey. You sound like old Bass Reeves. He was always telling me I'd gotta pull myself together, make a new start, the Bible-thumping buzzard.'

'Bass Reeves, who's he?'

'A black marshal. He was my lover-man for a bit 'til he fell for li'l Stagecoach Mary, one of his own breed. Wouldja believe it, he went an' married the li'l bitch after she got outa jail.'

'That's funny you say that, Pearl, because we're supposed to be on the trail of a black sheriff, Otis McGee. He ain't a friend of yours, too, by any chance?'

'No, never heard of him. What's he look like? Bass is built like a bare-knuckle prize-fighter. Biggest man you seen.'

'No, this one's young, slim, not bad lookin', I s'pose, in his way – uppity nigra, got a lot of mouth.'

'Well, there's plenty of 'em in the Nations now. There were twelve thousand slaves freed after the war by the tribes, an' they been joined by others coming in from Arkansas to join 'em in that string of coloured towns this side the border. You know, them at Langton are talking about startin' their own university. They really gittin' organized.'

'Who told you all this?'

'Bass. And my mother told me that the legal position of blacks in this territory was never made clear in the reconstruction. Whether the baddies should be taken back to Fort Smith for trial before the Hanging Judge, or be subject to Indian tribal law. What you gonna do when you arrest him?'

'Shoot the bastard, that's what we'd do. But Vince reckons he's high-tailed it outa the Nations by now. So, we're just relaxing awhile. *We* ain't on the lam. Mind you, we ain't angels, neither. We work for Carol Lindeman as his hired guns, and he wants him dead. So now you know.'

'Now I know,' Pearl smiled, muzzily, opening her eyes. 'It's funny how much a man'll tell ya in bed. No wonder my man-hungry ma did so well. She was known as The Fixer. I do believe that in her younger days the Hanging Judge himself was under her spell. That's why he never sent her down for more than a few months even though Belle Starr was the most famous lady outlaw ever known, or infamous perhaps.'

'Belle Starr was your mother?'

'Sure,' Pearl smiled, proudly. 'And Cole Younger's my daddy. He's doing life.'

'Where is Belle these days?'

'Jesus! Where you been, Reno? Ain't you heard?

She's dead. My brother, Ed, shot her from ambush. Least, thass what he told me. He hated her. They were having an incestuous affair. She seduced him. It ain't uncommon in these parts.'

'Yuk! That's sick.' Reno gave a whistle of disgust. 'His own mother!'

'Yeah, but don't worry.' Pearl smiled up at him, simperingly. 'I ain't like that. I'm a sophisticated lady.'

'Really?' Reno glanced at her, the paint-smeared mouth, the disordered curls, her flabby bare arms, her drugged, drowsy eyes. Somehow she didn't seem as enticing as the night before. 'You coulda fooled me.'

Marina pushed through the door, a cigarette dangling from her lips, two mugs of coffee on a tray. 'There's a coupla shots of whiskey in both,' she muttered, sitting down on the bed. 'It's gonna be a real hot day out there.'

Reno took his time downing the coffee. It certainly had a kick. As he listened to their small talk he took his hunting knife from the holster hung over the bedpost. 'Hey, honey,' he drawled, poking it into Marina's fleshy back. 'Git in here. I fancy a change.'

'Sure,' Pearl agreed. 'Gives me a break. You boys still got some credit left. Have who you like.'

The chubby Marina giggled, disrobing and clambering in between them. She leaned over Pearl to stub out the cigarette, kissing her on the lips as she did so, then turned back to Reno and rolled into his arms. 'How ya want me, big boy?'

Seven

The little 'Katie' engine had blown a gasket, or something like that. The engineer himself didn't seem sure. All he knew was he was losing power and it was impossible to go on. 'What you going to do about it?' a travelling snake-oil salesman in a top hat and checked suit angrily demanded as the engineer crunched past on the gravel track below.

'I'm gonna shin up a telegraph post and send a message back to Wichita in Morse code. You folks better make yourselves at home. We could be here all night.'

Oh, no. Violet Thark's heart sank. It might be a cliché, but she actually experienced that sensation, her heart sinking inside her, as she contemplated the prospect of being stuck on this crowded little train all night. It was not the fact that she had no food, or drink, that she was unprepared for such an emergency. It was the thought that she would have to try to sleep through the night with these two repulsive, maniacal hunters in too close contact. She knew Coonskin and his mate, Jake, were maniacs. She could see it in their eyes, their nudges, their sniggers. If only the coach wasn't packed, she might have moved to another seat. On the other hand, perhaps it was a blessing. What if she had been alone in this carriage in the dark with these two?

However, she tried to make the best of a bad job, stepped out from her seat, and spoke cheerfully to the other passengers, sitting on the arm of a seat opposite, chatting to a family group. They were Slavs, who, in very fractured English, explained they were going to Tulsa to work in the mines and oilfields. 'You go work there, too?' the wife asked, bobbing a baby on her knee. 'No.' It was too difficult to explain. 'Just visit.' She changed the subject, asking them, with amusing use of signs, where they came from, the children's names, anything to pass time, to avoid going back to her seat. The Slavs were very friendly, especially when she said her sister had been the town teacher. Yes, they had heard of her. A fine lady. 'No, not me, my sister,' she said. 'I'm afraid she's no longer there.' They pressed food upon her, omelettes and salads, oddly spiced, wrapped in linen, and a vicious liqueur, slivovitz, laughing when she winced. It was a convivial evening, but she knew, heart falling, that when the candles were extinguished, and just a single hurricane lamp flickered, she would have to return to her corner hemmed in by the two strange, smelly backwoodsmen.

'Been enjoyin' yourself?' Cookskin asked, removing his boots from her seat. 'I been listenin' to you nattering away.'

Violet nodded and gave them a brief smile. The slivovitz was strong and she soon drifted into sleep. It must have been a couple of hours after midnight when she awoke with a start in the almost darkened train: a hand was creeping up her leg beneath her skirt like an insistent giant spider. Violet was incapable of movement, as if paralyzed, as the hand edged up higher, reached the flesh above her stocking top. She was aware of a stench of halitosis and realized that Coonskin's head was not far from hers. He had moved over to sit in the seat beside her and had fallen over, as if in sleep, and was lying across her, his arm pushing her skirt up across her knees. Violet met the eyes of his friend opposite. They were brightly and lecherously watching. What to do? If she screamed, appealed to her Slavic friends for support, it would be a dreadful scene. Violet was more afraid of scenes, of being the centre of embarrassing attention, than a great deal more.

The hand was exploring higher up her thigh. Violet tried to draw back but she was hard up against the seat back. Higher it probed beneath the rim of her cotton pantalettes. Violet swallowed her fear. She had a mental picture of Coonskin's dirt-filled fingernails. Suddenly, she bucked, like a wild bronc, pushing him away. She jumped to her feet, climbed wildly over him and Jake's outstretched legs. She headed down the aisle, along a darkened corridor by a baggage compartment to the train's water closet. She let herself in and bolted the door. She stood trembling, looking at her reflection, palefaced, almost ashen, in the moonlit mirror. 'Oh, my God!' she whispered, 'Why ever did I come?'

Violet stayed locked in the little closet for what

seemed like hours. Suddenly there were footsteps, a rattling at the door, heavy breathing outside. She stayed silent, held her breath. "Is somebody in there?' a man's voice demanded. Violet whispered in reply, 'I'm ill. I'm sorry. I can't come out.' There was a muffled curse, but, whoever it was, opened a door of the train and jumped out onto the track. Violet stayed where she was until dawn glimmered and there were other, more urgent female demands to be allowed inside. She shamefacedly abandoned her hiding place and returned to her seat, stepping through the slumbering trappers. Coonskin was back in his place. He opened a bloodshot eye and winked.

About noon the next morning a relief engine arrived from Wichita and Violet uttered a silent prayer as, amid much bumping and grinding, it was connected up. It would push the train from behind, with the out-of service engine being thrust forward in front. Never had Violet felt more jubilant as the loco-motive got up steam and set them rolling once more. She could hear its stack blasting: Cha! Cha! Cha! cha-cha cha-cha cha-cha. . . . Soon her nightmare would be over. At least, that was what she mistakenly believed.

'This is how you stop a locomotive,' Jed Flinn yelled, as he used a stout branch to lever the rails to one side. 'You knock out the ties and move the rails over a bit, not too much or they might see it and slam on the brakes. Just enough to make the loco jump the tracks and shake everybody up.' He tossed the branch away, gasping from the effort and grinned, 'So, now you know, boys.'

'How long we gotta wait?' Eli asked.

'How do I know? We just wait, thassall.'

They had set off before dawn and followed the Coney River until they saw the trestle railroad bridge; they had followed the track a short way south into the woods and set their ambush.

'You all clean your carbines while we're waitin' and see you sixguns are charged,' Flinn snapped at his gang. 'Blue Duck, you see to the driver and engineer, if they're still alive. Eli and Tadpole, your job's to get all the passengers off the train and take any valuables they got. Any men on board, tell 'em to toss away their arms. Don't kill 'em, not unless they look like giving us trouble. Use your guns as frighteners. I don't figure they'll argue. You can tell 'em who we are. That should scare 'em enough.'

Eli Gritts gave a wide grin. 'Yeah, they musta heard of us by now.'

'Stick with me, you'll be famous, boy,' Flinn said. 'Me and Charlie, we'll take the baggage car. There'll probably be an armed guard, but we should be able to persuade him to come out with his hands up.'

'Hey, ain't it a pity we didn't bring no dynamite,' Charlie Gilpatrick yelped. 'We coulda blown the caboose sky-high.'

'Yeah, well, I weren't planning on stopping a train when we first set out,' Flinn replied, sourly. 'We'll leave the hosses in the woods over there for a quick getaway.'

'Where we gonna go?' Eli asked.

'Catoosa, where else? Whiskey and wild women, thass what I need 'fore we head for Kansas. I hear tell Belle Starr's daughter's got a parlour house there with the best-lookin' gals in the Territory. We're gonna paint that town red afore we go.'

'Yeah,' Tadpole giggled, 'and maybe with blood.'

'Hey, you boys just curb your itchy trigger fingers. It's one thing killing a few Injuns, nobody every got strung high for that, nor fer killin' a few nigras, either – but just remember that killin' a white man's a hanging offence, and Judge Parker's still holding his court at Fort Smith. We done pretty good so far, we don't want to push our luck. What I'm saying is, just curb your natural born killin' instincts, boys, unless you got no other choice.'

'Gee, Mister Flinn,' the Choctaw half-breed, Theophilus Tadpole, whined, 'you sure got it all figured out.'

Flinn glanced at him, unsure whether he was serious or trying to be funny. 'You better believe it,' he muttered. 'In this game you gotta cover every angle. We don't want 'em sending the dang cavalry after us. We've had our fun, boys, but it ain't wise to put too many noses outa joint. You savvy?'

'Yeah.' The pimply-faced Charlie, in his floppy-brimmed hat, nodded. 'Doncha worry, Jed. We won't kill anybody 'less, like you say, we have to.'

'Right,' Flinn said. 'Now I vote we brew up some coffee and settle down to wait.'

The railroad carriage and caboose were rattling along the track at a good pace, thrust forward by the new engine at the rear. The 'out-of-work' fireman in the front engine was taking it easy peering out of the cab. 'Hold your horses!' he shouted.

'What's the matter?' the engineer cried.

'The rail! Fer Chrissakes, brake!'

The engineer did so, the wheels, clamping, screeching and sparking as they slid on along the track. But they could not stop, propelled onwards by the powerful engine at the rear. The driver pulled on his steam whistle to give warning, but it was too late. They were on to the break in the rails, ploughing off the track. The first carriage was dragged skew-whiff with the engine. The first Violet knew was women's screams, a juddering shaking and smashing as the whole carriage turned on its side. It could only have been a matter of a few seconds but it seemed as if time had gone into slow motion as they tipped over and she was pitched across on top of the family across the aisle. She did a complete somersault and when the train finally crashed to a halt in a mass of saplings she found herself with her hand on somebody's face, upturned, her skirt over her face, her legs kicking to right herself, as the two trappers thrashed about on top of her. Finally, they all managed to get to their feet, brushing broken glass from their clothes, not much the worse for wear except being bruised and shaken, the children crying and the baby howling.

The window she had been sitting beside was now broken and above them. 'If we climb up we can get out through there,' Violet said.

'Yeah, wimmin and children first,' Coonskin crowed, and he and his pal offered a leg-up to the Slav, his wife and kids. 'You can climb down on them trees.'

'You're next,' he grinned at Violet, and they got

hold of her arms and hoisted her up.

Violet gave a shrill scream as she felt a hand groping where it didn't ought to grope. 'Don't,' she shrilled, and legs kicking, managed to hoist herself through. 'Really!' she said to herself, climbing down to the ground. 'What uncouth men. Is that all they think of?'

Other passengers were climbing out of the overturned carriages – one man bleeding profusely from the head, a woman with a badly cut face. The second carriage was only partly off the track, and the baggage car and rear engine intact on the line. A woman was screaming that her mother was trapped inside, but the old lady was eventually dragged out. Fortunately, the train had not been going at too great a speed and most of the passengers had escaped with minor injuries. They were counting their blessings, unaware that they were about to be hit by further misfortune.

'So, that's how you stop a train, is it?' Tadpole grinned. 'Makes a bit of a mess, don't it? Now they gone left their luggage inside, how we gonna git at their valuables?'

'Take whatever they got on 'em,' Flinn snarled, gripping his sawn-off shotgun. 'Come on Charlie.'

The passengers suddenly became aware of the five gunmen emerging out of the trees, their arms aimed threateningly at them. Their moaning and complaining suddenly ceased as Eli Gritts fired two shots from his revolver over their heads. 'Howdy, white folks,' he called. 'Your troubles is just startin'. Anybody who argues gets it in the guts from me, personally. We want you lined up nice and tidy. Anybody with a weapon toss it away now, or else try me. I'm ready.'

Several men reluctantly produced sidearms from their belts and threw them down. The dark-faced, long-haired breed and his young black accomplice did not look the kind of men you argue with.

'Right, that's better. Now git your wallets and purses ready to drop in this gunny sack. We want everythang you got. Anyone tries to hold out on us gits his or her jaw broke for starters. Understand?'

Meanwhile Blue Duck was covering the engineer and fireman beside the rear engine, which was standing steaming and hissing, its stack still smoking. Jed and Charlie had gone to hammer on the door of the caboose. The eyes of the guard appeared at a barred window slit. 'You better unlock this box, mister, you hear?' Flinn shouted. 'Or we'll start pumpin' lead through these wood walls.'

'All right, boys,' the guard wheedled. 'I ain't gonna give you no trouble. Take it easy.'

They heard him unlocking, and when he appeared in the doorway, a uniformed employee, with grey hair and a sick expression, he thumbed behind him 'The payroll's in that trunk in there. There ain't nuthin' else of value.'

'That'll do us,' Charlie hollered, hauling him down and thrusting him away into the weeds.

He climbed into the wagon, Flinn close at his heels. Charlie shattered the trunk's lock with a revolver shot and hoisted the lid back. 'Jeez!' he cried with awe, seeing the wads of greenbacks. 'You were right. It's pay day for us.'

'Quick, stuff some of these into your pockets,' Flinn said to him. 'Don't let on to them other three dumbclucks. Why should they have the same as us? We were the ones who planned this, weren't we?'

'Sure, Jed,' Charlie giggled. 'Too dang right. Anyways, they can keep what they git from them passengers. Hey, this is doozy. I never seen so many dollar bills afore.'

When the two outlaws had stuffed as many of the wads of notes as they could into the pockets of their trousers and jackets, shoving others inside their shirts, they tipped what remained into a sack and jumped back down to the track.

The passengers were cowering back against the overturned train as Eli and Tadpole neared the end of the line. The two trappers had retrieved their skins from the carriage and Violet's small travelling valise. They stood on either side of her, protectively, their hunting rifles laid at their feet. 'This is all we got,' Coonskin drawled. 'We ain't got no cash, not 'til we sell 'em.'

'You sure about that, you smelly varmints?' Eli asked, but they certainly didn't appear prosperous. Nor the kind he would particularly want to aggravate. 'Who's she?'

'She's my niece. She's come a'visitin' her old uncle. She ain't got nuthin', neither.'

'Oh, yeah? Hand over that bag, sister.' Eli grabbed the valise and tipped its contents on the ground: soap, hairbrush, toothbrush, her nursing tin of first aid equipment, clean blouse, skirt and underwear, a New Testament and a leatherbound medical dictionary. 'Load of junk' Eli growled, kicking it aside. 'Come on, what else you got, or shall we give ya a strip search?'

Violet produced a purse from her skirt pocket. 'Only some silver, but please, I need it.'

Eli's strong white teeth gleamed. 'Yeah, so do I.'

Violet had a modest amount in dollar notes folded inside a secret pocket of her pantalettes and was frightened the black youth might carry out his threat. He had a wild, rolling-eyed, reckless air.

'Yeah, less take a look at the pretty white gal,' the breed, Tadpole, urged. 'She's lying, you can tell.'

He got his fist into Violet's luxuriant hair and dragged her out of the line while Eli kept the trappers covered.

'What's going on?' Jed Flinn called as he, Charlie and the Cherokee, hurried back down the track.

'We're jest gonna take a poke at this purty gal, thass what we gonna do,' Tadpole said, dragging the girl towards the woods. 'She's holdin' out on us. We gonna have ta strip her nekkid.'

'Aw, come on,' Flinn shouted. 'What did I tell you? We ain't got time to mess with her. We got the damn payroll. We're gittin' out. There's plenty gals where we're going.'

'Aw, hail,' Tadpole moaned, 'I never git to have no fun.' Viciously, he hurled Violet away and she tripped, hitting her head as she fell against the trunk of a tree. The breed hurried after the others. 'We better watch them,' he hissed at Eli, 'or we won't git our fair share of that payroll.'

Violet, concussed by the fall, was lying propped

against the tree as the two trappers watched the gunmen go, then picked up their rifles and wandered over to see how she was. 'I suppose I ought to thank you for trying to protect me,' she said.

This seemed to amuse Coonskin and his pal, who began mock-punching each other and hooting with laughter. Coonskin knelt down beside her and patted her head. 'Pretty gal, you sure say the funniest thangs.'

Over at the derailed train the two engineers and both firemen were talking to the passengers. 'We're gonna walk into Catoosa along the rail. Any of you don't want to come, stay here. We'll be back with a relief train. But it's gonna take some while.'

The passengers looked around at the gloomy woods, where bear and mountain lion might well prowl, and decided to go along, even the old lady and the man with the bloody head.

'We're going to try to make it to Catoosa,' one of the drivers yelled over to the two trappers. 'Are you coming?'

'Sure,' Coonskin grinned. 'We'll be along. Little gal ain't feelin' too well.'

As the passengers and railroadmen began to troop away Violet tried, dizzily, to get to her feet, holding onto the tree to steady herself. 'Wait for me, please,' she called, but her voice was faint and unheeded. 'I want to come with you.'

The trappers in their filthy buckskins were standing before her, cutting off her path to the railroad. She met the contempt in their jeering eyes and tried to scream. But before she could do so Coonskin sprang on her, clamping his palm across her mouth, pressing her head against the tree. He watched as the party of people trailed away around a bend in the track and they were left alone. 'It ain't no use screaming, pretty gal,' he leered, his gleaming eyes up close to her face. 'We're all alone. There ain't nobody gonna hear ya.' And he and his companion, Jake, began dragging her back into the depths of the woods.

The black sheriff and the white sheriff, alerted by gunshots in the distance, were riding their broncs at a hard lope along the railroad track towards Catoosa when they saw the wreckage of the train. 'What the hell's happened here?' Brick Brady asked. 'Where is everybody?'

Suddenly there was a piercing shriek from deep in the woods. Otis McGee whirled his horse around. 'What the devil was that?'

'Sounds like a gal in trouble.'

'We better go take a look.' Otis spurred his Appaloosa into the brush, weaving through the trunks of the tall firs.

Suddenly he was upon them in a small clearing, a white girl down in the dirt, her skirt up, kicking and wriggling, sobbing and begging, a greasy-looking trapper in a coonskin cap, kneeling on top of her, his buckskin pants around his knees, his hams bared, slapping at her with one hand, pulling a knife to prick at her throat with the other. 'You wildcat, I'll teach you to scratch and bite,' he hissed. 'I'll cut out your lights. When I'm through with ye, that is.'

Another equally villainous-looking trapper was standing watching, a rifle in his hands.

'Get off that filly,' Otis said. 'I do believe she don't welcome your attentions.' He held his horse steady as Coonskin froze and turned to see who had arrived. 'And cover yourself up. You ain't a pretty sight.'

As Coonskin hauled up his pants and stepped away from the girl, the other trapper swung his hunting rifle and fired. Luckily the Appaloosa moved at that moment and the ball scorched Otis's cheek. He whipped out his shoulder-hung Frontier, cocked, aimed, fired, all in one fluid movement, the explosion rapping out, the slug hitting the trapper in the chest, bowling him over.

At the same instant he saw from his eye corner the Coonskin raising his arm, the flash of a knife. Brady charged into the clearing, firing his carbine at the man. Coonskin gave a scream, his face contorted, slowly dropped the knife, and tumbled to the ground.

Otis studied the staring-eyed trappers in their frieze of death agony. 'They ain't gonna bother nobody no more.'

'Thank God,' Violet whispered, staring at the bodies.

'You all right?' Otis jumped lightly from his horse and knelt by the girl. There was horror in her eyes as she tried to crawl away,. 'It's OK. I ain't gonna hurt ya. I'm a lawman.' He gently put out his hand and stroked her tousled hair away from her eyes. She was half-sitting up, staring at him now, as if petrified. Her dress and bodice had been torn apart and her ample breasts were protruding from it. Otis could not avoid feeling a judder of lust, himself. He wanted to touch them with awe. But, instead, he whispered, 'Here, we better put them away,' and began to button her torn dress.

Otis looked up at Brady on his horse, but he, like the girl, seemed to be in a state of wordless shock. He was pointing a finger at her, his mouth open, trying to say something, but only able to stutter. And he began to back his horse away.

'What's the matter with you, Brady? Ain't you seen a damsel in distress before? Toss me that whiskey bottle you got in your saddlebag.'

'No . . .' Brady was stuttering and pointing – 'it's Eunice . . . Eunice Thark. But it can't be. She's dead.'

'Well, this one's very much alive.' Otis could feel the warmth of her beneath his hands as he finished buttoning her up to the throat. 'Come on, gal,' he coaxed, touching the bruise on her cheek. 'Tell Sheriff Brady. Tell him your name. He thinks you're some ghost.'

'I'm Violet,' she whispered, huskily. 'Violet Thark.'

'You're Eunice's sister?'

She nodded, staring into the trees. 'Yes. They murdered her. They would have murdered me.'

'That's a possibility.' Otis squeezed her hand. 'But they didn't. And them two didn't kill your sister. You're fine. Come on, let me help you up. You cain't sit here all day.'

'Please.' She gripped his arm. 'Don't leave me.'

'We ain't gonna. We'll see you into town. Find you a hotel. You got any cash?'

'Yes. They didn't find it. Why?'

'So, you can pay your way. What you doing here out on your ownsome, anyhow?'

'I came to find out who killed Eunice. She was my twin.'

'Your twin.' Brady gave a gasp as he took a nip of whiskey. 'I *see*. For a moment there you gave me a fright.'

He tossed the bottle to Otis who caught it and gave it to the girl. 'Here, take a sup. It's against the law, but I won't arrest ya. It'll put some fire in you. You've had a shock.'

Brady smirked. 'Wrassling with them two filthy varmints would give anyone a shock. Did they do anythang to ya, gal? I mean did we arrive too late?'

'No,' she whispered. 'I'm all right. I fought them off. But they would have if you hadn't arrived.' She coughed on the fiery liquor, but forced it down. 'Yes, I think I feel better now.'

'Where are the other people?' Brady asked.

'They've gone towards Catoosa. I wanted to go with them, but—'

'Well, we better go after them.' Otis lifted her to her feet and climbed onto his saddle. 'Here, you better ride behind me.' He put a hand and swung her up to sit side-saddle. 'Ready?'

'Yes.' She nearly fell off as the horse gave a jolt, springing away with its double load. She grabbed hold of the young man's waist to steady herself. 'I'm sorry. Do you mind?'

'Nope. Help yourself. Snuggle up, honey. It feels fine.'

'Can I just stop and pick up my things? They're on the ground. Those thieves who stopped the train—'

'Thieves?' Brady shouted. 'What were they like?'

'There was a nasty dark one with long hair, and his friend, a black boy, and an Indian in a suit, and two white men, one much older than the other.'

'They robbed the passengers?'

'Yes, and they said something about a payroll.'

'Shee-it!' Otis whistled. 'It's them.'

'You know them?'

'Know them. I'd like to. But I don't think they want to know us. We've been chasin' 'em all round the Territory.'

'They can't be far ahead,' Brady said. 'Violet, you see which way they went?'

'Yes, they came out of the trees on horseback and headed towards Catoosa.'

Otis watched the girl packing her things into a bag as she knelt by the track, then he swung her aboard again. 'This time we might catch 'em.'

As they rode away Brady called across, 'For a man who'd never killed anybody before you certainly didn't waste time with that trapper. Did it occur to you that was a single shot rifle and he'd spent his bullet?'

'It did cross my mind, but it was too late then. Why, you think we shoulda taken him in?'

'Ha!' Brady gave a snort of incredulity. 'As they hadn't done nuthin' except attempted rape they would have claimed to be innocent. You glad you killed him?'

'The two resisted arrest. They deserved to be put down. Yes, I'm glad I killed him.'

The girl linked her hands around his waist and pulled herself into him, resting her head against his back. 'So am I,' she whispered.

Eight

Vince, Reno and the boys were feeling kind of jaded by the moonshine whiskey and Pearl's girls slick-fingered attentions. It was Sunday morning and Pearl was putting on a little bolero jacket over a fresh dress and pinning a concertina-shaped hat, topped with feathers and fluffy lace, at a jaunty angle of her raggedy brown curls. 'I gotta go to church.' She gave her mischievous dimpled smile. 'You boys better be on your way. The gals don't like working Sundays. You'll find plenty more drinking dives down along the wharves.'

'Church!' Reno drawled in awe. 'Just what kinda hypocrite are you?'

'We can go to church if we wanna. It's fun seein' the folks' faces when we flaunt in down the aisle. Anyhow we gotta keep up a respectable image, like I told you. These are the gals of my Ladies' Academy. I'm teaching them the fine arts.'

'Of fornication,' Heather giggled, wrapping herself in a black velvet topcoat and adjusting an even more flamboyant hat. 'Here y'are, boys, you had

110

a good time. You better pick up your guns and go.'

Marina gave a goofy grin, combing out her blonde hair. 'Yeah, we gotta give them gen'lemen worshippers the eye. Them storekeepers might be with their frosty wives but it won't be them they'll be lookin' at.'

'Pays to advertise,' Pearl cooed. 'My Ma taught me that. Anyway, we need a li'l outing, cooped up in here all day. Which reminds me, I gotta go put flowers on her grave. I gave her a big tombstone, carved like a hoss. She was a great rider. Better'n me.'

'Maybe you're a better rider in other ways,' Reno guffawed, as he strapped on his heavy gunbelt with its twin Whitney .36 calibre revolvers. 'Eh, gal?'

Suddenly there was a banging on the front door and they all froze. 'Who the hell's that?' Slim drawled.

Pearl went to her peephole, opening it a fraction. 'I don't like the look of 'em. Scurvy bunch.' She snapped it closed. 'Looks like a 'breed, an Injun, a black boy, and a couple white guys, one tall, one short. You know 'em, Vince? Take a look.'

The hammering had recommenced with vigour, the stout door shaking. 'Open up, 'fore we break you down,' a voice shouted.

Vince took a peep. 'Nope, never seen 'em before. But they certainly don't look like lawmen.'

'Yeah, they look like trouble. Writ all over 'em. Aw, guess I better explain how thangs are.' She opened the peephole wider and peered out. 'You quit that hammering. This is a young ladies' academy an' we're just off to church. Ain't you got no respect?'

'Naw.' Flinn's unshaven jaws split into a cracked

grin. 'That ain't somethang I ever had. Ain't this Pearl's place? We're here fer some fun.'

'This is the Lord's Day, our day of rest. Anyway, we don't open the doors to saddle tramps. My young ladies only entertain gentlemen of means and they have to be respectful.'

'Aw, cut the cackle an' open up. We ain't got much time.'

'Come back on Monday when y'all taken baths and bought some cleaner duds. We don't do business with bums.'

'Bums, tramps? What'n hell you talkin' about, lady?' Charlie Gilpatrick yelled, standing on tiptoes to peep through at Pearl. 'We're rich. Hey, look at this.' He stuffed a wad of greenbacks half-through and pulled them back out, quick, before they got snatched. 'The real McCoy. An', hey, who are them other guys I can see in there?'

'They're genl'men callers who stayed the night. They know how to treat ladies.' Pearl rubbed thumb and forefinger together through the hole. 'Let's take a look at that spinach. How do I know it ain't counterfeit?'

'Here, there's five of us. Take five hundred.' Flinn turned to Eli, Blue Duck and Tadpole, extending his palm. 'We gotta give 'em a hundred each, okay? They're playing hard to get.'

'A hundred?' Eli's voice rose high in awe. 'I generally git it fer free. Most I every pay is five dollars.'

'OK, cheapskate, stay outside. How about you two? I'm tellin' ya, this'll be worth every cent. We'll make sure of that.'

Reluctantly, the three others handed him their lesser share from the robbery, and he stuffed it through the hole.

Pearl took it, counted it, raised her eyes to the ceiling. 'Fools an' their money surely are quickly parted. Looks like we ain't goin' to church, gals. You git paid double-time.'

She returned to the peephole. 'OK, but you gotta give up your guns at the door, an' take a bath out back. My young ladies are very clean. They don't wanna catch no bugs.'

'A bath!' Charlie whined. 'Aw, hail, I had a bath last year.'

'Thass the deal. We gotta do as she says. We be good to them gals, an' they'll be good to us. This is a classy joint.'

'Come on in,' Pearl smiled, as she unbarred and unlocked. 'Those other *hombres* are just leaving. They'll guarantee you'll get a good time, eh, boys?'

'Yeah, heaven's gate they oughta call this place,' Arthur beamed. 'I thought I'd fallen among angels.'

'I ain't interested in angels,' Tadpole scowled. 'I want an angel who knows how to—'

'Aw, they know how to do that,' Reno snapped. 'These gals'll suck you dry and spit out your bones.'

'Yeah,' Hank agreed. 'They're worth every cent.'

'All you gotta do is behave yourselves,' Vince said, his thumbs stuck in his gunbelt. 'We hear of anybody gittin' rough we'll be back.'

'That's right,' Slim drawled, backing him.

'Oh, yeah?' Flinn growled, meeting Vince eye-to-eye. They stood there like two dogs, sniffing each other, hackles raised. 'An' who the hell are you?'

'That's none of your business,' Reno put in, touching the gutta-percha butts of his revolvers, a new idea that gave a better grip, and, unlike hickory, didn't get eaten by weevils. 'But to put your mind at ease I can tell you we definitely ain't lawmen.'

The two gangs stood facing each other, uneasily, in the crowded room. 'Come on, boys,' Pearl cooed, taking her hat and coat off, tossing out her curls. 'Hand in your guns and come into the parlour while we heat up the boiler for your baths.'

But Flinn wasn't satisfied. 'So, if you ain't lawmen, who the hell are you? What you doing in Catoosa?'

'You could say we're private guns for hire.'

'What, bounty hunters?'

'Nope, don't piss yourself,' Vince said. 'We ain't interested in you guys, whatever you mighta been up to. We're looking for a black sheriff. He comes from a town called Wild Cat. Seen any sign of him on your travels, boys?'

'Wild Cat?' Eli glanced sharply at Flinn. 'That'll be Otis McGee. He's sheriff there. I didn't think he'd take it lying down.'

'McGee, yes, that's him,' Reno said. 'We last saw him in Tulsa 'til he took off with some lump of lard calls himself a lawman, Brady by name.'

'You know,' Flinn said, scratching his jaw, 'I've had the weirdest feeling the last week that we were being followed and not far behind. So, it's McGee and Brady! Well, thanks for the warning, mister. If they come we'll be waiting for 'em. It's us they're after.'

'Whadda ya know?' Vince yelled. 'I knew all I had

to do was sit here and wait. Boys, you can be the spiders that lure the flies into our net.'

'What 'n hell you talkin' about?' Arthur asked.

'I mean we're on the same side,' Vince said. 'Come on, men. Let's git. You fellas enjoy yourselves. We'll be over the road waiting for McGee and Brady and watching your backs. You hears any shooting, come out guns smoking whatever you might be up to. And I wouldn't drink too much of that Knock-'em-Dead moonshine. It don't improve the aim.'

As Carol Lindeman's men clattered out and Pearl locked up, Jed Flinn winked at his boys. 'Looks like we got back-up. Hand in your guns like the li'l lady says. Sooner we get washed the sooner we git on with it. I could do with a shave and change of underwear. Hey, Pearl, why don't you send one of your gals down to the store and git us some fresh duds?'

'They ain't open on Sunday.'

'Aw.' He flicked her another couple of hundred in bills. 'They see this cash, they'll soon open up.'

'I could do with some new boots.' Eli pondered the flapping sole of one of his. 'These are coming apart at the seams.'

'By the smell of you you could do with some new socks, too,' Pearl smiled. 'Don't worry, boys, by the time we get you freshened up and smellin' of roses Otis McGee won't recognize ya.'

When Otis and Brady caught up with the train passengers straggling along the line, Violet jumped down and found her medical aid kit in her bag. While the two lawmen questioned the engineers, she bandaged the bloody head of a man who had taken a bad tumble in the crash, and attended to other minor abrasions. The old lady was in a state of exhaustion, so Brick Brady hoicked her up behind him.

'So you got yourself a galfriend at last?' Otis grinned across at the white-haired toothless crone in black widow's weeds who had her arms hooked around Brady's corpulent belly. 'You'll be all right with him, missus. It's time he had somebody to attend to his bodily needs.'

'Shuddup,' Brady growled. 'Save your breath. You may be needin' it.'

'Have a bullseye, Granny.' Otis offered her the sticky bag of striped sweets. 'Doncha worry, his bark's worse than his bite. I think he likes ya. I bet he ain't had a female so close in a long time.'

Violet, riding behind McGee, gave him a dig in his waist with her knuckles. 'Don't be so awful.'

'I've told you, loudmouth.' Brady turned, pointing an aggressive finger, his knobbly-potato face burning. 'You just keep them wisecracks to yourself or you and I are going to have a falling-out.'

'Aw, I'm only joking.' Otis put another bullseye in his cheek as he guided the Appaloosa along the track. 'But tell me, what does a bald-headed ole bachelor like you do for sexual titillation? You gotta do one thing or another. Or are you past it?'

'That ain't none of your business, smartmouth. Every dog has his day, and I've had mine I can tell you.' Brady glared across, his pudgy face even redder. 'When you git to my age it ain't something you got on your mind incessantly like you damn—'

Violet quickly butted in. 'Don't take any notice of him, Mr Brady. He's just teasing you.' She knuckled Otis in the ribs again, studying his handsome face, his blue velvety jaws, the crinkly black hair, the chocolatey pigmentation of his supple neck. She had never been so close to a black fella before and there was something about this one curdled her insides. 'Leave him alone,' she whispered.

'You fancy one of these gobstoppers, gal?' Otis offered the bullseyes back to her. 'No? Maybe it's somethang else you like to suck on?'

Oh, my God, Violet thought, he's as bad as the others! So, it was true what they said about them? Why did men always pursue her? Just because she was young and was termed well-appointed, with a rather ripe hour-glass figure, they flocked about her like bees around a honey pot. When she had met Otis's dark brown eyes, gentle and concerned, as he comforted her back in the woods she had hoped she had at last met a man who cared about her as a person, for herself, for her mind. But it seemed, from the cracks he made, he just saw her as some sex doll, lusting superficially for her like all the others. She loosened her hold around his waist, tried to balance on the horse more circumspectly. What could she have been thinking? She shook her head, tried to pull herself together. It was, in fact, unthinkable that a respectable white young lady should throw herself at a black fella, slim and handsome as this one was; it verged on the blasphemous, or would do in the minds of the mid-southern white majority.

It would only be asking for trouble for both of them. No! Violet took her hands away from the black sheriff as if his touch might burn her. Impossible! She would do what she came here to do and get back to civilization. But when the horse stumbled crossing the rail she gave a squeal and grabbed hold tight of Otis again. And, as she hung on, she could not deny the pleasant tingling sensation it gave her to hang on close to him. Just enjoy this experience, she told herself, and then it's over.

Brady had been sulking in silence for a while as they rode, but he asked, as the iron bridge over the Verdigris River came in sight, 'Where you reckon they'll be?'

'Waal,' Otis drawled, 'where would you be if you'd been out in the hills for a couple weeks an' you had a pile of stolen gold burning a hole in your pocket? No, maybe *you* wouldn't. But me, I've an idea these boys will make for the classiest whorehouse in town. They'll just love to splash their cash around.'

'Pearl Starr's?'

'Yes; you know it, Mr Brady?'

Brick flushed brick-red again. 'Not personally. But I've heard it's a den of iniquity.'

'Not to your taste, eh?'

'Quit the crap, McGee. What are we going to do? That's what I'm asking. What's the plan of campaign?'

'How should I know? There's five of them and two of us. We'll just haveta think of something on the spur of the moment and hope Lord Jesus is on our side.'

'Yeah, but what if He's busy?'

'First we gotta drop these ladies off someplace so they can tidy up and git themselves some vittles. That OK with you, gals? Maybe you could take my dang dawg with ya 'fore he gits shot?'

'My daughter should be waitin' fer me at the railroad station,' the old gal piped up. 'She'll be wonderin' what's happened to me. I'll tell her what a nice considerate man Mr Brady is. You call in at our place – the Mason ranch – any time, Sheriff, and have a piece of my pecan pie.'

'Yeah, put in your thumb and pull out a plum,' Otis smiled. 'I think the lady fancies you, Brick.'

The old lady clung to Brady and fluttered her eyelids. 'He is rather cuddly. I ain't been so close to a man in a long time. I was feeling down back there, but I'm all perked up now.'

'That's nice to hear, ma'am,' Brady muttered. 'Once we git to the other side of this bridge perhaps we're gonna have to drop you off to make your own way to the station 'cause things may well be hotting up for us.'

'You mean lead's gonna fly, Sheriff?' the widow squeaked as the two horsemen picked their way along the track of the bridge, its iron girders studded with rivets as big as a man's head. 'Lend me yer carbeene. I know how to shoot.'

'No, you better be hurrying along, Granma,' Brady said, as he reached the town side and lowered her down. 'This is man's work.'

'So long, Violet.' Otis offered his arm for the girl to swing from the Appaloosa. 'It's been nice knowin' ya.'

The young woman, in her torn candy-stripe, clutching her bag, and the hound, stood looking up at him with a distraught air. 'Am I going to see you again?' she asked, her eyes, involuntarily, brimming with tears.

'That's fer the good Lord to decide.' Otis seemed preoccupied with what he had to contend with, eyeing the wharves, drinking dens and boats along the riverbank, and the ramshackle false fronts spilling along on either side of the single track which headed on through towards Tulsa. 'Today is today and tomorrow is tomorrow,' he muttered. 'We'll jest have ta see how the clouds roll by.'

'Ha! You don't say!' Brady gave a derisive roar. 'Today's today an' tomorrow's tomorrow. What kinda profound philosophy's that, black boy?'

It was Otis's turn to growl, 'Shuddup.' He nudged the Appaloosa forward beside the rail, his eyes alert as he examined every door, window or possible hiding place for ambuscade. He drew his Creedmore .44-100 calibre carbine from the saddle holster and eased the safety catch off, pumping a slug into the breech. He held the gun in his hand as he rode.

'Ha!' the old lady screeched. 'Them two. I like the way they drop us without a by-your-leave. They mighta bought us a drink 'fore they rode off.'

'Goodness.' Violet's lips trembled as she watched the two lawmen head on into town. 'I'm worried about them. I do believe they're in mortal danger. Take care, Otis. Take care.'

'Heck!' The old woman glanced at her, deprecatingly. 'I saw the way you was hanging onto that nigra.

You better get any fool ideas like that outa your head, gal. Come on, let's go.'

Violet shook her head and stumbled after her feeling strangely forlorn. They went along the track towards the town hotel.

Nine

'I ain't sure where her place is.' Otis and Brady had ridden slowly along the main street looking for Pearl's. There was not a lot of life in the town, it being late Sunday afternoon. But, ignoring God's ordinance to rest from their labours, some men were lethargically loading bales onto barges and flatbottoms down at the levee and they had heard female shrieks and drunken caterwauling coming from the dives along the waterfront. A few farmers and ranch hands were sitting out in the sunshine on the veranda of Shelley's Hotel, smoking and jawing after a late Sunday lunch. A small bunch of children were playing with hoops and skipping ropes or sitting in the dust. And they could glimpse family parties inside the restaurant.

The bystanders watched, curiously, as the young black man and the bulky, double-chinned white man rode by, possibly wondering why they had weapons clutched in their fists. But most folks – Indians, white settlers or railroad men – were probably indoors out of the heat, taking the chance of an afternoon snooze.

Otis tossed a quarter to one of the kids. 'Where's Pearl's place?' The Indian boy snatched the coin and smiled, knowingly. 'Along there, mister. Two white cottages. Opposite O'Reilly's emporium. You can't miss it.' The rest of the children giggled, envious of the boy's luck, as the two riders jog-trotted on, alertly.

There was a goods train and its 'puffing Billy' silent outside the railroad depot, the open trucks loaded with barrels of oil. The iron track in the centre of its dusty street then dipped down an incline on the left-hand side of which was the block of two white-painted plank cottages, a door at either end. There was a sloping shingled roof and smoke trickling from a chimney. 'That must be it,' Brady said, noting there were no horses hitched outside, but maybe they had been taken into the low stabling around the side. 'It's all quiet.'

Otis gritted out, 'Not fer long it ain't gonna be.'

'You see anybody?'

'Nope.' He had halted the Appaloosa and swung it around to examine the double-storeyed clothing and general goods store across the way. A crudely painted sign in crimson said, simply, 'O'Reilly's'. It appeared to be Sunday-closed. But suddenly Otis saw movement behind the curtain of a half-opened window upstairs and a rifle barrel sliding sinisterly out. 'Watch it!' He swung his carbine up and snapped off a shot, smashing a window. There was a yelp and the rifle disappeared from sight. Almost immediately men with carbines and revolvers appeared at other windows of the store, but by then Otis and Brady had skittered their horses back along the street a piece, whirling them around to fire at the gunmen in the store.

Bullets were whistling and whining back and forth, so far, at such range, to little effect. But suddenly the windows of Pearl's cottage were smashed from within, there was the sound of female screams, several desperadoes showed themselves, guns flashing and crackling in their fists, and Otis and Brady found themselves caught in a crossfire, a proverbial hail of lead. Otis swung the Creedmore in a traverse, aiming at each of the cottage windows in line, pumping his lever, shooting from the hip, But Flinn's gang continued to give as good as they got. 'Uh-uhn!' Brady gave a gasp as a bullet powered through his side. He fell forward hanging around his bronc's neck. 'Argh!' he groaned. 'Gawd!'

'Hang on!' Otis hauled his Appaloosa around and grabbed hold of Brady's reins, setting off, hooves kicking dust, bullets hissing about him, back up the incline. He leaped from the Nez Percé mare, catching Brady as he fell from his saddle and hauling him under the guard's van of the goods train. They lay there breathing hard, as slugs clanged against the wagon wheel, or ricocheted hither and thither. 'That was a close one. There's five of them in the store. And I counted five of them firing from the windows and doors of Pearl's.'

'I'm finished,' Brady coughed out. 'You better get outa here, man, while you can.'

'I ain't goin' nowhere jest yet.' The black sheriff of Wild Cat pushed Brady back into the shelter of a wheel. 'Let's see what the damage is.'

Brick Brady watched, a sickened look on his puglike face, with his knobbly, whiskey-veined nose and little eyes beneath shaggy brows. 'Don't bother 'bout me, Otis. Save yourself. The odds of you staying alive are ten to one against.'

'Who the hell are them others?' Otis tore Brady's vest and shirt away from his fleshy abdomen. The undervest of pink flannel was sodden with dark blood. He tore that away, too. 'Well, what do y'know?' He studied the round hole in the whale-belly white flesh from which blood was pumping. 'It looks like it's gone clean through.'

'That may be a good thing.'

Otis gave a start as he heard Violet's clear, sweet-toned voice. 'What are you doing here?

'I heard the shooting, came to take a look.' She slid in beneath the goods van beside them. 'Here, let me see. Yes, I think you're right. He may be in luck if it's missed the vital organs.'

'You call this luck?' Brady groaned. 'I need this like a moose needs a hat-rack.'

Violet could not help smiling at his quaint expression and the alarmed look on his face. 'Lay back, Mr Brady. You'll be all right. I've brought my medical kit. I'm going to try to patch you up. Otis, put your fist on this patch while I bandage him. We've got to try to stop him losing too much blood.'

Otis watched with awe as the girl expertly bound his partner's bleeding side, neatly pinning the bandage tight. At the same time he kept glancing out from under the van to the two wooden buildings just down the hill. But all was quiet. They were lying doggo, no doubt waiting for him to return to the attack.

'OK, you bastards,' he gritted out through his teeth. 'I'll be back.' An idea had formed in his head. 'Violet, you do your best for Brick. He's my buddy. I don't want to lose him. And give me all the spare bandages you got.'

'What for?'

'Just gimme 'em, thassall.'

He snatched at the bundle of bandages she offered him, and muttered, 'Wish me well, pal,' before slithering away.

'Yeah,' Brady grunted. 'And you me.' He tried to force a smile at the girl. 'He's got a nerve, that boy. What'n hell's he up to?'

'Don't talk,' she hissed. 'Lie back.' She laid her hand tight on the wound. 'We've got to stop the flow.'

'Look what you done to my furniture!' Pearl was screaming at the Flinn gang, pointing to her bullet-pocked wallpaper, the broken glass littering her oriental carpet, the smashed vases and knick-knacks. 'I knew I should never have let you madmen in here.'

Flinn and his boys were kneeling by the windows and open doors, carbines hugged into their shoulders. 'Ah, stow it, sister,' he snarled. 'Quit your yappering. Brady's had it, but where'd that black fella get to?'

'Let's go look for him?' Tadpole shouted, flicking his long hair out of his eyes, his dark, half-Indian face determinedly set. 'You with me, Eli?'

'Sure.' The black boy's voice quavered. He wasn't

as eager as Tadpole. He had heard about Otis McGee's ability with a gun. 'Why'd I drink all that durn whiskey? It's made me go weak at the knees.'

'Weak in the head is all you are,' Charley Gilpatrick guffawed. 'Go on, git out there, but take care. Keep in the shadows.'

'We'll be covering you, boys,' Flinn said, shaking his head, wishing that he, too, had not imbibed so much Knock-'em-Dead. It had not assisted his aim, which was probably why their shooting had been wild and McGee had got out of there. He forced himself to concentrate, mind over matter, gripping his Smith & Wesson. 'Try to draw their fire.'

Over at O'Reilly's emporium, O'Reilly and his wife were similarly remonstrating with the gunmen. Vince Hope and his men had swaggered in that Sunday morning, after banging for them to open up. They had a couple of Pearl Starr's hussies with them, ostensibly buying clean shirts and pants for some customers of theirs. But Vince and his gunmen had hung around playing poker all day, making it clear that the O'Reillys were, virtually, their prisoners. And, then, in the afternoon the fat one, Arthur Simms, had shouted a warning that McGee and Brady were riding up the street. Arthur had slid his rifle through the net curtains, taking a bead, as the others rushed to take a look. But, before he could fire he had been flung back, taken out by the black sheriff's first shot. Now his corpse lay on the O'Reillys' bedroom carpet amid a dark pool of blood, flies buzzing about it.

'I never knew a man had so much blood,' Mrs

O'Reilly shrilled as she tried to mop it up. 'Why don't you get outa here, leave us honest folks in peace? On a Sunday, too. What will folks say?'

'Yeah, boys, they've gone now,' her husband cried, looking at the broken window glass. 'Why don't ye get after 'em, it's no use staying here? You missed your opportunity, indeed you did.'

'That black's up to something. He'll be back,' Vince drawled, as he leaned against the wall, craning his neck to peer up the hill. 'There's two of them other creeps, the black and the breed, sneaked outa Pearl's. Let them take a look first. We already lost one good man.'

'Aw, he ain't got a chance,' Reno hissed. 'There's still nine of us against one nigra.' He got to his feet, hitching up his cross-hung revolvers. 'I'll go give 'em a hand.'

'Take care, Reno,' Vince said. 'I got a feeling that nigra's on a lucky streak.'

'Ha!' Reno gave a snort of contempt. 'What the hell you scared of? I can take him with one hand tied behind my back.'

When Reno got out into the street he saw Eli Gritts and Theophilus Tadpole flitting like dark shadows up the sides of the street, dodging for cover behind piles of pig iron rails, felled trees and heaps of refuse left to rot in the sun. Reno strolled after them, taking the centre of the street, his fingers spread over the twin Whitney .36's on his hips, his hawkish face alert. He was looking for a straight gun duel, confident he could best McGee.

The black sheriff had hefted two of the barrels of oil from one of the goods trucks. He was busy prising out the bungs with his knife and stuffing twisted bandages in, soaking them in oil to act as fuses. He was concentrating on the task when he glanced up and saw Reno walking up the dirt hill. And he was obviously looking for a showdown. Otis swallowed his alarm, and rose to meet him, trying to wipe the slimy crude oil from his hands onto his suit. It had put him at a disadvantage.

'OK, black boy, say your prayers,' Reno called. 'I'm coming to get you.'

Otis straightened up, holding his ground, pulling his jacket aside with his left hand, raising his right hand waist-high. 'I'm ready,' he muttered, 'when you are.'

Reno had his straight-brimmed hat jammed down over his slits of eyes, his neckerchief fluttering in the slight breeze, his leather chaps swinging as he hip-rolled towards his adversary, looking every inch what he was – a professional killer.

Otis stood poised, coiled to snap into action like a released spring. Fifty paces away, thirty paces away, passing the goods van, Reno prowled towards him intent on getting in an accurate shot. Twenty-five paces. Reno went for it. Both hands brought out the .36's like greased lightning. The barrels belched flame and lead. Reno gritted his teeth.

Otis McGee fell back onto the dust, jerking free his Frontier a split second after him, thumbing the hammer, taking aim with both hands and firing as Reno's bullets spat over his head into the dust behind him.

Reno stood there for seconds, his harsh face splitting into a smile, but it was an agonized one. His silver-engraved revolvers dropped from his hands and he slowly spun around and collapsed into the dirt. 'Hot damn,' he hissed, looking at the blood oozing from his chest. 'You didn't play fair. You didn't stand up to me.'

'I ain't crazy,' Otis grinned, kneeling down beside him, as the gunman's head fell back. 'You cain't win 'em all, mister.'

He glanced around him. He thought he had seen a movement on his left behind a rubbish pile. The bullet creased his curls a split second after Eli showed himself, a Winchester carbine in his hands. Eli jumped forward, levering it for a second shot as Otis took careful aim and let him have it. The Frontier barked and Eli threw up his hands and back-pedalled to lie in the stinking rubbish. 'Oh, Chrissakes!' he cried. 'Don't kill me.'

Otis raised his Frontier for a finishing shot, but suddenly recognized the black youngster. It looked like he was badly wounded and out of action. He looked around him. He thought he had seen another movement, but maybe it was his imagination. 'Thass what you git fer robbin' and killin',' he shouted to Eli, and returned to his task.

Violet held her breath as she listened to the shootings. She lay beneath the goods van and watched Otis successfully defend himself. But now another man, the long-haired breed, had crept past her on the far side of the goods train to Otis, and he had a heavy Colt revolver in his fist. He had not seen her or

Brady. He had reached a gap in the trucks exactly opposite where Otis was kneeled busily over a barrel, his back to him, unaware. The breed was raising the Colt, taking careful aim, about to shoot the black sheriff in the back.

Violet snatched Brady's revolver, lay forward, balanced on her elbows, and squinted along the sights. She had never fired a gun before, but, fortunately, this one was already cocked. She had only to pull the trigger. She hesitated a fraction of a second, biting her lip, and fired. The sixgun kicked but the bullet powered out, knocking Tadpole off his feet as his own Colt crashed out fire.

Otis spun around, alarmed, reaching for his Frontier, but Tadpole was down on the ground screaming and sobbing, clutching his torn shoulder. Otis dodged through and disarmed him, then met Violet's violet eyes. His white teeth flashed in the sunlight. 'I guess I owe you one.'

'Don't leave me here,' Tadpole pleaded. 'I'm bleeding to death.'

'Shuddup. I'm busy. Where are the others?'

'Back in the cottage.'

'Right, relax. She'll wetnurse ya.'

Otis found a tin box of lucifers in his pocket, rolled one of the barrels forward to the brow of the hill, lit the fuse, and kicked it forward. The oil barrel went bouncing down towards Pearl's cottage, banging against the side wall. For moments he thought the short fuse might have failed. But, no—

'Whoomph!' The oil exploded into flames and black smoke, bursting through the thick plank walls, licking upwards to the bedroom window. 'Got ya!' Otis yelled in triumph, and ran back to the second barrel. He rolled it forward, lit the fuse and set it rolling towards O'Reilly's emporium. His aim was good – or lucky. Whatever, the barrel lodged against the outer wall and he waited for the explosion. The oil went up, blasting a hole in the wall, its flames immediately catching the tinder-dry planks. 'Take that!' Otis grinned. 'That should flush the lousy rats out.'

Townspeople had come running to see what the hullabaloo of gunfire was about and gathered behind Otis, watching. 'Get them kids outa here,' he yelled, 'and all of ya get back. There's gonna be bullets flying every which way any minute. That's unless any of you men want to help apprehend some dangerous lawbreakers. I could do with a hand.'

The crowd of white folks, men, women, children, and Indians, backed away to the sidewalks and stood sullenly watching.

'OK,' Otis yelled. 'It looks like I'm on my own. Violet you better get out of the way, too. There's still seven of 'em and I ain't sure I can hold 'em.'

The girl watched tense-faced as he pulled his carbine out of the saddle holster and sent the Appaloosa skittering back along the main street for safety.

He reloaded his Frontier and checked the magazine of the seven-shot carbine, then ran from the shelter of the goods van to take a position behind the pile of pig iron. 'Let 'em try an' get me. Come on you bastards!'

Pearl's was by now blazing merrily and she was the first one to run out, holding her gramophone, with its big horn, in her hands. Her hair was smoking, and she put the playing machine down and started to slap at her head, dementedly. Finally, she dunked it in a horse trough. Pearl ran back into the house shrieking, 'Get the piano out,' but Flinn pushed past her, one arm around the exquisitely-dressed Heather's throat, propelling her in front of him, his S&W Safety Hammerless in his right fist.

Charlie Gilpatrick followed him, an arm around the dumpy Marina's waist, his Colt Thunderer pressed to her temple. The stumpy little outlaw peered over her shoulder from beneath his floppy hat and yelled, 'Who's got the last laugh now, huh?'

Blue Duck was the last to appear, stern-faced in his high-bowled hat with its single feather. A revolver ready-cocked, he was holding Pearl tight in front of him as a shield, as she kicked and screamed, 'The cash! The cash! My money's in there.'

'Aw, shee-it!' Otis held his Creedmore tucked tight into his shoulder, squinting along the sights, but he was reluctant to chance a shot that might hit one of the terrified girls. They might be bad, but they didn't deserve to die. And no man in the West, no man of honour, cared to kill a female.

His dismay was doubled when he saw Vince Hope step out of the emporium emulating Flinn's lowdown tactics, holding Mrs O'Reilly across the front of him, while the gangling Hank Martin, in his buckskins, followed pushing old man O'Reilly forward, his arm twisted behind his back. Slim appeared behind them, but as Otis took a snap shot at him he dodged safely for cover behind a rubbish pile. Otis fired again and sent a tin can flying.

Now the five men, with their human shields, were moving slowly up the slope, slinging lead as they came, making Otis duck for cover as the slugs hissed dangerously close.

'All right, McGee, throw your guns out and show yourself. You ain't got a hope in hell,' Flinn shouted in a lull in the fusillade of lead. 'We'll forget about this. You can go on your way.'

'I ain't so stupid, Flinn,' Otis yelled back. 'Put them wimmin aside an' I'll come out shootin'. You lousy cowards, you have to hide behind wimmin's skirts?'

'You're finished, McGee. We got these hostages' – Flinn shook Heather by the scruff of her neck – 'and we don't give a damn if they die. Their deaths'll be on your head.'

'Git fugged!' Otis loosed a shell from his powerful Creedmore that cut the feather from the Cherokee's hat. But, as they instantly returned fire he had to dodge back again. He looked around him for other cover and saw Slim with his knife raised about to throw. He levered, thumbed the hammer, squeezed the trigger and fired as the knife cut through his shoulder. Slim was catapulted backwards by the shell and lay back against a wagon wheel, his arms splayed as the blood pumped from his heart.

Otis crouched like a hunted animal as the gunsmoke rolled, for what could he do about those five killers and their sneaky tactics? They were getting closer and closer, silently, keeping their ammunition in their revolvers ready for the kill. He could almost see the colour of their eyes as they climbed up the hill. 'Give yourself up, Sheriff,' Pearl pleaded, her blue eyes bulging with terror. 'If not, they'll kill us. They really will.'

What could he do? It looked like to save the hostages he would have to sacrifice himself. Or get out of there quick.

Ten

The Prince of Hangmen, they called George Maledon. In his time at Fort Smith he had personally attended to the trapdoor demise of sixty felons condemned to death by the Hanging Judge (who would watch approvingly from his office window), and shot four who had attempted to escape his noose. He was as expert with the pair of pistols he wore on a belt tight around the waist of his grey suit as he was with a rope. A strange, staring-eyed man, with a jutting, moth-eaten white beard, he was at that moment riding from Tulsa towards Catoosa with Deputy Marshal Bass Reeves.

'Sounds like trouble,' Bass sang out as he heard the sound of explosions, the gunfight raging in the ramshackle port town ahead of them. Smoke and flames were billowing from the first two of the houses. 'Somebody's setting the town afire.'

'There's always trouble in this hellhole,' Maledon called out, reaching for one of his revolvers and spurring his horse forward. 'Looks like business calls, Bass.'

The big-shouldered black marshal whacked his

sturdy blue mule forward at a stiff-legged canter – he swore by a mule for stamina over a horse any day, but it was a tad lacking in the speed department – and reached forward to draw his saddle gun, a long-barrelled Volcanic. 'After him, boy,' he shouted.

Bass had been dispatched from Fort Gibson in response to an urgent telegraph message to attempt to apprehend two homicidal escapees from Arkansas state prison – Jed Flinn and Charlie Gilpatrick. Judge Parker had stressed that they must be taken alive and returned to Fort Smith. In Redwood he had bumped into George Maledon, who, it seemed, was doing a bit of moonlighting, or extra-legal hanging. The two had had a certain contretemps before, or falling out, but bygones were bygones, and they were now the firmest of friends.

Maledon was sitting his horse, watching the battle, when Bass caught up. Five gunmen – with three girls, an old man, the storekeeper, O'Reilly, and his wife held in front of them – were pushing their way up the slope, firing at what appeared to be one lone recipient of their fury. They were blamming away with such enthusiasm, noise and gunsmoke, they failed to notice the arrival of the black marshal and the hangman.

'It always was Sodom and Gomorrah,' Bass intoned, touching the crucifix at his throat. 'Perhaps we should let this town be put to the flames?'

'If you ask me, those are the fellas we're after.' Maledon had filled Bass in on what had occurred at Wild Cat according to Otis McGee. 'And that might well be the black sheriff himself, one of your own.'

'In that case, vengeance is not only the Lord's but mine,' shouted Bass. 'Charge!'

'Don't shoot to kill. Remember what the judge said,' Maledon howled. 'I need my hanging fees.'

Vengeance certainly was theirs as they raced to the rescue. Bass Reeves put a bullet into the Achilles heel tendon of Hank Martin that made him drop Mrs O'Reilly like a hot brick and go hopping and screaming away. As Vince Hope swung round to face him the Volcanic roared again, Bass's arm out-stretched, and Vince was knocked into the dust, his broken thigh pouring blood.

Jed Flinn released Heather and turned, his face expressing sour disgust at the sight of the bearded hangman riding towards him. He raised his Smith & Wesson, but he was too late. The hangman's lead shattered his wrist and the double-action went spinning away.

When Charlie Gilpatrick let go of Marina, he took aim at the white-bearded apparition. But the irate prostitute kicked him in the shin which made him fall back and miss. Maledon swung his bronc around and fired with deadly accuracy into Charlie's upper shoulder. 'You had enough?' he thundered. 'Toss that gun away.' The pimply Charlie thought twice about it, but when he met the hangman's maniacal eyes he surrendered the Colt Frontier.

Blue Duck, however, was made of sterner stuff. He kept Pearl tight to him and began gobbling like a prairie turkey – the Cherokee death chant – and advanced on the black man on the mule, wildly emptying the cylinder of his revolver at him.

Bass winced and ducked, trying to aim his Volcanic at arm's length but worried about hitting his former lover, Pearl.

Suddenly, the Cherokee threw up his arms and fell to the ground, dragging the girl with him. Otis McGee showed himself, his Creedmore smoking. He had put Blue Duck down with a neat shot through his side. He gave a wide grin and trotted down the hillside to them.

'Any more for any more?' Bass roared, whirling his mule, and thumbing the Volcanic half-carbine, still ready for battle.

'Whoa down, boy,' Maledon shouted. 'I think them that ain't dead have had enough.' His eyes gleamed. 'They got an appointment with me at Fort Smith. These sort are all yellow-bellied cowards underneath. We'll see how they perform on the scaffold.'

'Git him off me.' Pearl was kicking pantaletted legs trying to detach herself from the Cherokee who was holding her in his death hug. 'Help!' she screamed.

Otis broke the dead Blue Duck's hold and hoisted her to her feet. 'Hiya, honey,' he grinned. 'You're safe now.'

'Yeah, safe to come back with us under arrest,' Bass boomed. 'I've warned you before about the wages of sin, Pearl. You haven't heeded me. At least your house of shame has been put to the flames, praise be the Lord.'

'Aw, shut up, Bass, you mealy-mouthed dingbat. You've enjoyed yourself in there before now.' Pearl looked close to tears as the town fire brigade raced their hose and tender up. 'There's all my cash and clothes and stuff in there. You gotta save it.'

'Don't worry about that filthy harlot.' Mrs O'Reilly began tugging at the chief fireman's shirt as he began pumping water. 'Save my store. We're not insured.'

Otis shrugged and smiled, and left them to it, walking back up the hill, his Creedmore over his shoulder, to see how Brady and Violet were. The young woman was climbing from under the goods wagon and her smile was as wide as his as she saw him. She didn't care about the folks milling about them, running to rubberneck; she hardly noticed them. It was as if she and the black sheriff were the only two people about, and she ran forward and flung herself into his arms, hugging him and, finally, offering her lips to be kissed by his.

The dead – Reno, Slim, Arthur, and Blue Duck – were dragged over to the sidewalk and with Bass, Otis, and Maledon standing behind them, weapons in hand, had their picture taken for posterity by the town photographer. He huddled under his black cloth calling to them to get closer in, and popped his flashlight

The wounded – Flinn, Charlie, the 'breed, Tadpole, Eli Gritts, Hank and Vince – were lifted, groaning and cursing, into one of the goods vans, and tended to, to the best of her ability, by Violet. After a while, she wiped her hair from her perspiring brow and said there was little more she could do.

'Let me see to your shoulder now,' she said to Otis McGee.

'You've worked wonders none of 'em deserve,

honey,' Otis smiled. 'You go across to the hotel and get cleaned up. We got a few questions to put.'

'I think, that one,' she hissed, pointing to Theophilus Tadpole, 'may be the one. I found this around his neck.' She showed him the green jade Cherokee god. 'It was my sister's. She always wore it. And when I look into his eyes I get a creepy feeling, as if Eunice is talking to me from the dead. We were very close.'

'Yep. I think he may be our man, although' – Otis pulled at his lower lip, thoughtfully, eyeing Tadpole – 'I ain't sure. You run along.'

When Violet had jumped down from the goods van, Otis slammed the door closed and stepped over to the long-haired Choctaw breed. He pulled his knife and began to hack at his hair. 'I been asked to take your scalp back to a certain Pawnee chief to show that young Indian gal you raped and killed is being avenged.'

'Hey!' Tadpole squealed with fright, for like the Indians he was inordinately proud of his hair and shared their superstitious belief that it was his power. 'You can't do this.' He groaned at the shot wound in his side inflicted by Violet, and appealed to Bass and George Maledon. 'This ain't legal. He can't do this. I'm a wounded prisoner. I got rights.'

'He can do just what he damn-well likes,' Bass snapped. 'If I was him I'd take your whole damn scalp.'

'Yes,' Otis dug his blade into the back of Tadpole's head. 'Why not? An eye for an eye. A life for a life. I think I will.'

'No!' Tadpole screamed, trying to hold him back. 'Leave me alone.'

'You killed that Pawnee gal and her brother, didn't you?' Otis slit the scalp so blood began to flow. 'Didn't you?'

'Sure, why not? You cain't hang me for that. They's only Pawnees. They ain't whites. Hey, I'm bleeding. Stop him, Marshal.'

'You killed the white girl, Eunice Thark, outside Tulsa, didn't you? You pulled that charm from her neck.'

'No, I didn't kill her.' The breed's voice was rising shrill with fright. 'Please, don't! When we found her she was already dead. Or just about. Hardly breathing. She had no hope.'

'He raped her,' Eli said, holding his bandaged chest. 'So did Charlie. It was sick. She died as they done it but they still went on.'

Flinn hugged his shattered wrist and spat out, 'I told 'em to stop, but they took no notice of me. Hell, it's true, she had been killed by somebody before they even began.'

'You can't be tried for raping an already dead woman, can you?' Charlie asked, in a shaky voice. 'That ain't fair.' He studied his bandaged shoulder, already beginning to seep blood. 'I admit to killing them Osage police but they can't hang me for that.'

'What about my friends – Henry Smith, the butcher, and Sam Stevens, the bank teller at Wild Cat. Who gunned *them* down?'

'That was Flinn,' Charlie said. 'And he killed the Osage chief.'

'Ah, shut up,' Flinn snarled. 'We were in it together.'

'Yes, you're all in it together,' Bass drawled. 'I'm going to draw up charges and transport you back in irons to Fort Smith. Meanwhile I'd like you to think on the words of Samuel: "How are the mighty fallen! Tell it not in Gath, publish it not in the streets of Askelon; lest the daughters of the Philistines rejoice, lest the daughters of the uncircumcised triumph. . . ." '

'Aw, no,' Charlie wailed. 'He ain't gonna give us religion?'

'Amen,' Otis sang. 'Mr Reeves here will take care of your souls and Mr Maledon your necks. How about you other boys? You ain't saying much, Vince? Maybe it was you killed that white girl?'

Vince Hope lay on the floor, his broken leg in splints. 'You can't pin that on me, black boy.'

'Well, you tried to pin it on me, dincha? I figure you and Hank are going to look mighty nice kicking air. What if I tell the people in Tulsa it was you and hand you over. Just 'cause you an' Hank cain't walk no more it won't stop 'em putting ropes around your neck. Them miners can git mighty irate – I know, from experience.'

'Go on,' Hank shrilled. 'Tell him, Vince. I ain't taking the rap for that. We ain't done nuthin' 'cept obey orders from *him*.'

'Him? Carol Lindeman?'

'Yes, he dunnit. He beat her senseless,' Vince said. 'He told us to dump the body on the trail. That's all we did.'

'She wasn't dead, the breed here says so. She was

still breathing. You might have saved her.'

'No.' Vince made a grimace. 'That blow on her head. She looked as good as dead to us. I'm sorry. OK, I'm a hired gun. But I liked her. Everybody did. I didn't want this.'

'Save the sob-story for the judge. You all going to make statements to Marshal Reeves here tomorrow. Me, on behalf of Sheriff Brady, whose jurisdiction it is, I'm gonna go see what Carol Lindeman's got to say. Come on, boys. Talking to these scum makes me feel sick. Let's go eat while I still got an appetite.'

They jumped out of the goods wagon and slammed the door, locking it. 'Waal,' Otis sighed. 'That's that. I'm gonna go git in a hot tub.'

'Yeah, man,' Bass laughed. 'Go wash the dirt outa your soul. This is a lousy job we're in, but somebody's got to take a stand. Stand up for the Lord. Alle-loo-yah, yessuh!'

'Alle-loo-yah,' Otis grinned, slapping his hand. 'You know, if liquor weren't banned in this Territory I might jest take a glass tonight. Thass the way I feel, Just this once.'

Maledon patted his back and smiled through his beard. 'You might just be in luck, boy. My theory is if you don't sell it to the Indians then there's no harm in it.'

'I don't think Judge Parker would agree,' Bass said. 'But you got a point, George. I might break the rule myself. A man needs to liquor when the Lord's work's been done.'

'And maybe, if Pearl and her girls could consider staying at the hotel to help us celebrate this victory for law and order, perhaps,' Maledon suggested, his eyes twinkling, craftily, 'we could drop the charges against her. After, all, the poor girl's lost her house and her cash.'

'That might be charitable,' Bass agreed. 'The Lord is a forgiving God. I don't know what Stagecoach Mary would say, but she's at home with our child.'

'What the eye don't see, the heart don't grieve, as the motto goes,' Maledon said, hitching up his holsters and striding across to Shelly's Hotel where they had Pearl and her hussies locked up. 'You think she'd object to me, seeing as how I'm, you know, a hangman?'

'Aw, no, George. She's a professional lady. I know Pearl from old,' Bass smiled. 'She'll be glad to join the party. She's like her mother, a chip off the old block.'

'Jeez!' Otis watched them go, giving a whistle of awe. 'Those guys! Talk about hypocrites.' And he sauntered away to the bath house.

'Waal,' he sighed, as he sank into the suds, 'I guess I can't blame 'em. We all need to unwind.'

Eleven

'Maybe I'll have the pleasure of hanging you one day if you go on the way you're going, Pearl,' George Maledon said as he, Bass and the girls stumbled up the hotel stairs at midnight.

Otis McGee grinned, widely, as he lay in Violet's bed. 'Ole George is a cheerful sort. He sure knows how to woo a gal.'

Violet kneeled over him in her nightdress, touching with awe the perfectly proportioned planes of his shoulders, his smooth brown chest, studying the wide ovals of his eyes, the dark smouldering irises and pupils with their touch of blue, his flared nostrils, expressive lips, fine white teeth and impish dimple in his cheek. 'You're so beautiful,' she whispered, 'you don't need to sweet-talk a gal. I bet you've had hundreds, haven't you?'

'Not hundreds, a few.' He squeezed her bare arms. 'Never one like you.'

Violet listened to the mumble of men's voices, the squeals of the girls in the adjoining rooms, and murmured, dreamily, 'I never thought I'd lose my virginity to. . . .'

146

'A *negro*? Yeah, it might be a kinda shock to your folks when you introduce me.'

'I feel wonderful,' Violet smiled, her mass of curls tumbling across her brow as she straddled him and felt him beneath her. 'I can't understand why some women make so much fuss. Suddenly I feel free.' She pulled her nightdress over her head and tossed it away, pressed his dark hands to the magnificent globes of her breasts, whispering, 'Shall we do it again?'

'Waal,' Otis grinned, his teeth flashing in the candlelight, 'it don't sound like we gonna be given much chance to sleep.' And he pulled her face down to his lips. He wanted to be more gentle with her this time, but he gave a snort of laughter mid-kiss when he heard through the thick plank wall the rapid groaning of bedsprings. 'Just hark to old George going at it as fast as a fiddler's elbow.'

Violet's body shuddered with helpless laughter as she collapsed on top of him. But pretty soon their own iron bedstead was creaking with the same contrapuntal rhythms as those on either side.

The cock had long ago crowed by the time Otis tucked in his newly-washed shirt, clipped on his shoulder holster and went down to breakfast of steak and eggs. 'I need to keep my strength up if I'm staying with this gal,' he grinned.

Bass was busy trying to sort out his accounts. 'You think she will be agreeable to come into Fort Smith as a witness?'

'You'd better ask her.'

'If she ain't I'll have to subpoena her. Don't wanna do that. Let's see now. This here gold coin's what I figure was stolen from the Osage treasury.'

'You better leave it with Sheriff Brady. The quack says he better lay up for a bit. But he'll see they get it back.'

'Can we trust him?'

'Course we can trust him. He's solid as a rock.'

'These greenbacks must be from the train robbery, property of Lindeman. They look newly minted. If you're going looking for him, you'd better take the cash with you. Can I trust you?'

'Of course you can trust me. It's the miners' wages. What do you think I am?'

'Thou shalt not steal. Always obey the commandments, Otis.'

'Like you – what about thou shalt not commit adultery?'

Marshal Reeves frowned. 'The devil tempted me. We are all sinners, Otis.'

'We surely are. The flesh is weak,' Otis laughed. 'Well, mine sure is this morning.'

'The rest of this cash, these wallets and baubles must be what they stole from the train passengers.'

'Brady'll see it gets back to 'em. How about the money they stole from my people at Wild Cat? Four hundred dollars from the bank, and two hundred from the tobacco warehouse.'

'Sorry, Otis. There ain't nuthin' left.'

'You mean I've chased 'em all around the damn territory—'

'They musta spent it.'

'What on?'

'Guess,' Bass mumbled, as he spotted Pearl, in her hat like a concertina, her little jacket and long dress, swishing into the restaurant. 'Howdy, Pearl. Where you been?'

'I've been poking through the ashes of my academy and guess what?' she said, brightly, waving a metal cash box. 'Look what I found.'

She sat down beside them and began to pick through its contents. 'I'll have to pay this into the bank. There's some bad hats around.'

She held up a bunch of notes in one hand as she poked through the coin. 'Hey, that's mine,' she protested as the marshal took it from her.

'No, it ain't. It's stolen money.' Bass counted out six hundred dollars and gave it to Otis, fending Pearl off with a strong forearm as she fought to try to snatch the cash back. 'That belongs to the folks of Wild Cat. The rest, let's see, we've got three hundred dollars left. Perhaps me and George and Otis should share this to reimburse us for all our trouble.'

'Nah, I don't want it.' Otis put up his hand to push it away. 'That's daylight robbery.'

Pearl seemed to agree for she was cursing like a trouper as she struggled with Reeves, calling him every name under the sun.

'Let's look at it this way, Pearl,' Bass's deep voice rumbled out. 'A deputy marshal gets only six cents a mile for expenses while trailing an outlaw, a two dollars arrest fee, ten cents a mile to feed and transport himself and his prisoners back to Fort Smith. I won't tell you how small our salary is, you'd only laugh. For that we're supposed to put our lives on the line. So I say these wages of sin ought to go towards doing the Lord's work saving the hides of honest folk.' He tucked the notes into his pocket and smiled at her. 'Case proved?'

'Aw, let him have it, Pearl,' Otis said. 'After all, nobody ain't gonna pay this ugly mug to go to bed with them, like they do you. I 'spect you got plenty left in the bank.'

'That ain't the point,' Pearl smouldered. 'I'm a business lady.'

'So, look at it as an investment in God's work,' Bass smiled, winking at her. 'After all, by rights I oughta take you in.'

'Pah, you lousy cheatin' lawmen and preachers, you're all the same.'

'What's going on?' Violet asked, as she joined them.

'Nuthin' much,' Otis replied. 'Have some coffee, honey. Stack up on steak and eggs while I go buy you a horse.'

'Have a nice time last night, Violet?' Pearl asked, simmering down when Otis had gone. 'You sounded like you did.'

A strawberry blush spread to Violet's pale cheeks as she sat dressed demurely in a clean blouse and skirt. 'Yes, thank you. The best of my life.'

'Really? Would you be interested in working for me? It's good money.'

'No, thank you.' Violet poured herself black coffee from the jug. 'I'm a one-man woman, I'm afraid.'

'You an' Otis thinking of gittin' hitched? That

would sure make people's eyes pop out.'

'I – I don't know. I haven't thought about it.'

'Well, you better had. If white folks hear what you been up to you're likely to git tarred and feathered and both run outa town. Course, it don't matter if you're a gal like me. You can have any man.'

'Leave her alone,' Bass growled. 'Violet's genuinely fond of Otis, anyone can see. And she ain't got no, wish to be a Jezebel, like you.'

When they had said their goodbyes to Brady, Bass and the hangman, Otis and Violet headed on their horses, bypassing Tulsa, across country towards Carol Lindeman's ranch house. It was dark by the time they reached there and they waited in the shadow of the trees watching as a lamp burned in what looked like the dining room of the low-slung one-storey plank house.

'I cain't see no signs of guards,' Otis murmured. 'Come on, we'll leave the hosses here, go take a look. You sure you're up to this?'

'Yes,' she whispered. 'I'm ready to try.'

'Good.' He led the way carrying his Creedmore. 'Careful now. We don't want 'em to hear us. I only hope they ain't got no dogs.'

They circled round the back of some stables and suddenly heard a man's voice inside, talking to the horses. There was the clatter of a bucket. Otis pressed himself against the wall by the door, signalling to Violet to stay back. There was a soft foot-fall on straw and the hired gunman, Logan, appeared. Otis let him pass and thudded him on the back of the neck with the butt of the Creedmore. He slumped to the ground, out like a light. Otis dragged him by his legs back into the stable, tossed away his gun, found some rope, tied and gagged him. 'Sleeping like a baby,' he grinned. 'Let's hope he's the only one.'

They made a quick dash across a strip of moonlit ground to the back of the house. A curtain was fluttering out of a half-open window. Otis peered in. It appeared to be the master bedroom. It was in darkness. 'In you get,' he said. 'Don't knock anything over.'

Violet touched his arm and swung over the sill. 'I'm scared.'

'Don't worry,' Otis hissed. 'I won't be far away.'

Further along the back of the house there was another lamp burning in the kitchen window. Otis took a peep and saw an Indian girl in a flimsy white-woman's nightdress and negligée of expensive embroidered silk. A black woman in a maid's black dress, white collar and cuffs was washing dishes. 'You and James can turn in now,' the girl said. 'I'll finish those. Mr Lindeman and I are going to bed.'

A black guy in butler's duds, penguin suit and white gloves, appeared and the girl ushered him and his wife out, calling 'Goodnight.' Otis stepped back and watched them amble over to their cabin in the trees. The Indian girl was about to close and bolt the door when Otis put his boot in the crack and pushed the door back. 'Not a word,' he hissed, jabbing the Creedmore into her.

Ice Along the River's mouth opened as if she were

about to scream, her eyes widening with fear, but she stayed silent. Otis touched his lips and beckoned her out of the kitchen. 'You're coming with me.' He grabbed her arm and hurried her across to the stable. He quickly roped her to a post alongside Logan. 'Please,' she begged, 'don't hurt us.'

He showed her his sheriff's badge. 'Don't worry, babe. I ain't gonna hurt *you*. It's your husband I want. Did you know he murdered Eunice Thark?'

'No, I didn't. I don't believe you.'

'Please yourself. He may not have meant to but he sure as hell did. Do you wanna hear what he says?'

Ice Along the River nodded, mutely, and Otis untied her. 'You promise you won't give us away?' She shook her head. 'Right. Come with me. Are there any more guards about?'

'No,' she whispered as she let him guide her back towards the house. They could see her husband inside the dining room. He was putting some writing materials and accounts aside, rising from the table, a burly, Slavonic man with thick black hair and pointed beard, stretching, yawning, looking around. 'He is wondering where I am.'

'He's gonna git a surprise,' Otis whispered.

Carol Lindeman left the room. They heard him open the kitchen door as they hid back in some bushes. 'Ice?' he called, looking out. 'She musta gone to bed,' he muttered and doused the lamp, bolting the door.

'Come on.' Otis hurried the Indian girl back along the side of the house to the open bedroom window. 'We're just gonna listen,' he whispered.

*

In that day and age a good many people strongly believed in the afterlife and Carol Lindeman, although professing to be a sceptic, when it came to the crunch was no exception. His hair literally rose on the top of his head when he entered his bedroom and saw the young woman sitting up in his bed. The chestnut curls tumbling across her brow, the wide-eyed stare, the sultry lips, the luminously pale skin of her temples and neck, the heavy bosom pressing out her white blouse. He dropped the oil lamp with his surprise. 'Eunice?' he stuttered. 'Eunice . . . what . . . why. . . ?'

'I've come back for you, Carol,' she hissed.

'No!' Lindeman pressed his eyes with his left hand. 'It's not possible.'

'I am here, Carol. I have come back for you.' The young woman rose from the bed, holding the sheet across her, speaking in an unearthly monotone. 'Why did you do this to me?'

Carol Lindeman backed away, holding his hand out, pleading. 'No, Eunice, please. Don't! Leave me!'

'Why did you hit me, Carol? I loved you. I was going to be your wife. Why did you seduce me? Why did you lie to me? Why did you kill me?'

By now Lindeman was gibbering like an idiot, falling to his knees, staring up at her. 'Please, Eunice, I didn't mean to. It was a terrible accident. I was angry.'

'You beat me across the face and head, Carol, didn't you? Don't you remember the blood?'

'No!' he shrieked. 'Yes, yes, I did. I mean, I hit you,

but, as you fell over you cracked your head on the fire grate. Don't you remember, Eunice? That's what killed you.'

'You half-murdered me, brutally, Carol, and even though I was still alive, you got your men to drag me away. They left me on the trail bleeding but still breathing. Then those other men came along and horribly raped me. Why did you leave me to them, Carol? Why didn't you help me?'

'I . . . I don't know. I didn't want to, Eunice. I panicked. Please forgive me.'

By now Violet was standing over him, the sheet draped across her. The kneeling man reached out his hands to her, imploring her, and half-expected them to pass through this vision. 'Forgive—' He gave a strangulated cry as he felt the firmness of her hips. 'Eunice? Is that you? Are you alive? What trick is this?'

'No, I'm not Eunice. I'm her sister.' Violet cast the sheet away from her. 'I've heard all I need to hear. I'll give evidence against you.'

'You—' Lindeman gave a strangulated cry and stumbled to his feet, reaching for her. 'You bitch. Where's my wife? What have you done to her?' He caught hold of her by the neck and began shaking her. 'You damned interfering bitch! How dare you? I'll kill you!'

Violet struggled to free herself, scratching the wild-eyed man across his face, but Lindeman seemed to have gone berserk. For seconds she believed he would really strangle her. 'Otis!' she screamed. 'Help me!'

Otis tumbled through the window, swung Lindeman around and smashed his fist into his face, sending him toppling to the floor. Lindeman grunted, 'You bastard.' He scrambled to his feet and dived across to the other side of the bed, opening a bedside table drawer. He had a German Luger-type pistol in his left hand when he turned and fired wildly at the black man, who ducked behind the bed. The bullets thudded into the walls. The oil lamp had spilled and spread; suddenly flames were leaping up the curtains. Violet screamed again as Lindeman turned the gun on her. Otis rose to his feet at a crouch, his Colt Frontier in his hand. It spat flame and bullets as he fanned the hammer and Lindeman went down, eyes staring, falling back against the wall. He slowly slid down to lie supine.

'My God,' Ice Along the River sobbed. 'You've killed him.'

'Yeah, I'm 'fraid so. It was him or us.' Otis grabbed hold of Violet and the Indian girl and bundled them towards the window. 'Come on. We gotta get outa here. This place is going up like a tinderbox.'

Flames were already scorching them as they climbed out of the window, smoke billowing out, choking Otis, the last one out.

'Jeez!' he cried, ducking away towards the stables. 'Look at it go. There's no way we can save it. Thass the last you'll see of that ole house.'

The two young women stood silently beside him watching the blaze. Glass was popping, flames reaching twenty feet high. Otis reached out and squeezed both their hands. 'Well, Lindeman confessed before he went, so maybe he'll rest in peace.'

When the flames finally subsided into a pile of glowing ashes they went into the stable and lay down in the hay. Logan had come to and was asking what had happened.

'Looks like you're out of a job, man. You, too, James,' Otis said, as the black man and his wife brought them cups of coffee. 'Sorry about this. He didn't oughta have dropped that lamp.'

They slept in the stable and in the morning Otis handed Ice Along the River the pile of dollar bills from his saddlebag. 'This is the payroll loot. You better take it in to Tulsa and give it to the miners. Anything left over, and whatever's in his bank is legally yours. What you planning to do?'

'I will go back to my people. I am glad I found out what he did. Thank you, Otis.'

'Well, we'll be moseying on. Ready, Violet?'

They called to the hound dog, climbed onto their horses and headed away at a fast canter, riding all morning until they reached the bank of the Verdigris River. They made a small fire and boiled coffee. Otis stripped off his shirt and boots and waded into the water watching and waiting for his chance. A quick grab and he came up with a rainbow-hued trout. Soon he had six gutted and lying in a pool. They fried them for lunch and, sated, lay watching some beavers paddling about their lodge. Otis tossed a fish and enticed one to him. The beaver proved quite tame and came waddling up onto the bank to take the fish. Otis reached out and patted its oily wet coat. 'Can you imagine anyone killing these li'l thangs?

They been hunted close to extinction. Luckily them funny beaver hats now gone outa fashion an' the beaver's on the way back.'

Violet smiled at him as they watched the animal paddle back to the lodge. She reached out a hand to caress his neck. 'Let's make love,' she said. Soon they were naked in the hot sun. . . .

'It's a good job nobody ain't around,' he grinned. 'They'd probably damned well shoot me.'

When they were through, Violet snuggled into him, staring at the rippling river. 'I've an awful feeling that was our last time,' she whispered.

'Why? Aincha coming to Wild Cat to be my bride?'

'Otis, you know I'd like to. But you know, too, it's impossible. The world isn't ready for us yet. You go back to your people. I'll go back to mine.'

'What if you should have a kid?'

A baby? It was not a possibility that had occurred to her. 'If so, I *will* be back,' she smiled.

They didn't speak a lot more, just lay and watched the river and the sun fall into a crimson haze. They dressed and saddled their horses and swung aboard. And each set off their separate way. Violet paused and turned in the saddle and waved. The black sheriff turned at the same time, raised his hand in salute, and loped on his way, the dog at his heels, around in a bend in the river until he disappeared into the trees.

Afterword

As for Sheriff Brady he took the Cherokee's and Tadpole's hair, plus a photograph of the dead outlaws to show the Pawnees that they had been avenged. He returned not with Light on the Mountain, but with her mother, Pennahwenomi, as his squaw.

Jed Flinn, Charlie Gilpatrick, Eli Gritts and Theophilus Tadpole, when they had recovered, were hanged side by side on the scaffold at Fort Smith. They drew a record crowd.

Vince Hope and the remainder of his men received six months imprisonment for attempted murder of a lawman.

The little town of Tulsa became the oil capital of the Western world and the Osage tribe the richest in the States. Today they can be seen turning up at the annual corn-reaping powwow in their ornate robes, most of them driving Cadillacs.

The Indian nations were later assimilated into Oklahoma – which, ironically, means Land of the Red Man. It is one of the most culturally diverse states in the USA – Italians, Slavs, Indians and Black people mingling there. This story was a fiction but was based on fact.